Lily Palmer's To-Do List

—Get Dr. Cullen Dunlevy's house—and
  foster kids—under control

—Stop the children from creating "potions" in
  the bathroom and putting rubber snakes in
  my candy

—Bake Christmas cookies together—as a family

—Stop thinking about Cullen's—I mean,
  Dr. Dunlevy's—sexy dimples...and how cute
  he is with his children

—Hang the mistletoe—right where Cullen
  can see it...

—Decorate the tree with the kids to create the
  best holiday ever

—Have a forever family with the man—
  and family—

CELEBRATIONS, IN

D0956174

Dear Reader,

The Sound of Music has always been one of my favorite movies. I saw it for the first time when I was about four years old, and I make a point to watch it at least once a year. I never tire of watching Captain Von Trapp and Maria fall in love. In fact, the movie inspired the story *A Celebration Christmas.*

What's better than witnessing a strong woman and a gaggle of kids teach a gruff alpha male about the power of love? In *A Celebration Christmas,* Lily Palmer helps Dr. Cullen Dunlevy realize that not only is falling in love not a weakness, but that it's also the ultimate strength. In return, Lily finds the family for which she's been longing.

I hope you enjoy reading *A Celebration Christmas* as much as I enjoyed writing it. Please drop me a line at nrobardsthompson@yahoo.com and let me know what you think.

Warmly,

Nancy Robards Thompson

A Celebration Christmas

Nancy Robards Thompson

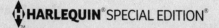
HARLEQUIN® SPECIAL EDITION®

Recycling programs
for this product may
not exist in your area.

ISBN-13: 978-0-373-65850-3

A Celebration Christmas

Printed in U.S.A.

NANCY ROBARDS THOMPSON

Award-winning author Nancy Robards Thompson is a sister, wife and mother who has lived the majority of her life south of the Mason-Dixon line. As the oldest sibling, she reveled in her ability to make her brother laugh at inappropriate moments, and she soon learned she could get away with it by proclaiming, "What? I wasn't doing anything." It's no wonder that upon graduating from college with a degree in journalism, she discovered that reporting "just the facts" bored her silly. Since she hung up her press pass to write novels full-time, critics have deemed her books "funny, smart and observant." She loves chocolate, champagne, cats and art (though not necessarily in that order). When she's not writing, she enjoys spending time with her family, reading, hiking and doing yoga.

This book is dedicated to Kathleen, Lori,
Cindy, Kathy and Mary Louise.
Thanks for always being there.

Chapter One

Cullen Dunlevy had never begged for anything in his adult life, but right now he was desperate. "I'll pay you triple your salary if you'll stay for two more hours, Angie," he said. "And you don't have to clean up after the kids."

"Dr. Dunlevy, there isn't enough money in the world to make me stay." Unmoved, the housekeeper brushed past him. She paused at the top of the stairs. "Call me when you find a home for *them*."

A home for them? They're kids, not stray animals.

Cullen glanced down at ten-year-old Megan Thomas. All the color had drained from her already pale cheeks. Then his gaze found its way back to the hall-bath toilet, which was overflowing with some kind of expanding blue goop that seemed to be growing exponentially. The prank had been the final straw, the reason for Angie's noon phone call to Cullen at the hospital, informing him he had exactly one hour to get home because she was fed up and leaving.

What happened to the theory "it takes a village"?

Couldn't Angie have a little heart? Sure, the four of them were unruly, but anyone with an ounce of compassion could see their disobedience stemmed from grief.

The kids had lost both their parents in a car accident. Their dad, Greg Thomas, had been Cullen's lifelong friend. Given the lingering sting of his own grief, he couldn't imagine what the kids must be going through. They were homeless and alone in the world except for each other. And they were at the mercy of the Texas Department of Family and Protective Services.

A pang of guilt coursed through Cullen. He had room for them in this big, empty house, but was that enough? Didn't kids deserve two loving parents? He was married to a job that demanded sixteen-hour days. He worked and slept, only to get up day after day to repeat the routine. He didn't know anything about raising kids. Hell, he'd thought he was doing the right thing by leaving them with Angie.

Obviously that had been a colossal mistake.

Standing there, alternating glances between Megan and the creeping blue foam, Cullen realized if he were any further out of his element he might sprout fins and gills and start flopping on the tile.

He swallowed an expletive and reminded himself that he might not be the best candidate to parent his friends' children, but the one thing he could do to honor Greg and his wife, Rosa, would be to make sure the kids stayed together. The kids would live with him until he found the right family that would take all four of them.

In the meantime, he needed to convince Angie to stay just a little longer.

The kids ranged in age from five to ten years old. They were relatively self-sufficient. In other words, Angie wouldn't be warming bottles and changing diapers. Just one more hour—give or take a few minutes—during which she could go on about her usual housecleaning duties, toilet-clogging blue foam exempted, while he interviewed Lily Palmer, the nanny candidate. At least Lily had agreed to change her schedule and move up their interview to one o'clock that afternoon.

Until he'd explained his dire straits, she hadn't been free until the end of the week. At least she was flexible. Of course, he'd cushioned the story, telling her that his temporary child care had fallen through and he was in a pinch. There was no way he was going to scare her off with the gory details of pranks and temper tantrums. He prayed to God that she was right for the kids and available to start immediately.

"I'm sorry, Uncle Cullen," said Megan. Her eyes brimmed with unshed tears. He'd known Megan and her brother and two sisters since birth. Hell, he'd known their father since the two of them were in kindergarten. *Uncle Cullen* was an honorary title that he didn't take lightly, especially now that Greg was gone.

"I told George not to dump the potion in the toilet," she continued earnestly.

Nine-year-old George was the second oldest after Megan, and he was conspicuously absent at the moment.

As chief of staff at Celebration Memorial Hospital,

Cullen ran a tight ship and prided himself on being unshakable even in the face of the most horrific medical emergencies. However, after taking in Greg's kids, Cullen had discovered he wasn't as unflinching as he thought.

But wait—

"The *potion?*" Cullen asked, Megan's words belatedly sinking in.

"Yeah," said the little girl. "We like to pretend we're scientists and the bathroom is our lab. We make potions out of all the things we find in there."

He tried to remember where Angie stored the cleaning supplies that produced noxious fumes if mixed together—like bleach and ammonia.

"Yeah, that sounds like fun," he said. "But it can be kind of dangerous. So you have to be careful. What did you mix together to make the potion expand like that?"

The girl had started to give him a laundry list of ingredients when Angie called from downstairs, "Goodbye, Dr. Dunlevy. I'm leaving now."

He'd let her go downstairs to cool off a bit, hoping he could talk some sense into her. Or bribe her.

"Angie, please wait."

He looked at the little girl. "I need to go apologize to Angie and try and talk her into staying. We'll talk about the potion later. In the meantime, please don't conduct any more chemistry experiments. And don't flush anything else down the toilet. Will you please make sure your brother and sisters don't, either? I'm counting on you, okay?"

Megan nodded and swiped at her tears. He ruffled her hair to show her he wasn't mad at her. He was mad at the situation, but what else could he do except go down and plead with Angie?

He was so out of his league. But when he'd gotten Megan's distress call three days ago, he'd had no choice but to bring the kids to live with him.

People could say a lot of things about Cullen Dunlevy, but no one could deny that he was a man of his word.

Six months ago, after Greg and Rosa's funeral, it seemed as if the kids were settled. They were set to move in with a great couple. Dan and Carla, friends of Greg and Rosa, had agreed to take in the kids—all four of them. They'd promised to love them as their own. But then Carla had gotten sick. Terminally ill. In the weeks before the adoption was to become final, they had to back out.

No warning. No opportunity for Cullen to point out that he wouldn't make a good guardian since he practically lived at the hospital. But he'd made a promise to Megan at her parents' funeral. He'd told her if she needed anything—anything at all—she could call him and he'd be there.

When he'd made that promise, he'd intended *anything at all* to mean money, a ride, advice. He'd never imagined the little girl would call, asking him to give her and her brother and sisters a temporary home.

But she had called, and he intended to keep his word for as long as it took to find the kids a new adoptive family where they could stay together—all four of them.

Cullen swallowed bile as he headed toward the kitchen to try to sweet-talk Angie into staying until he'd had a chance to talk to Lily. He and the kids would sort out the blue mess in the bathroom and their behavior later.

"Angie, will you please just help me out today? I'm desperate. I need you. Just until after the interview. And maybe to show the nanny the ropes. Then you're off the hook."

When Cullen had asked Angie to watch the kids, she'd made it very clear that her schedule was full. She'd built a nice business cleaning house for many of the doctors and professionals at Celebration Memorial. In fact, she delighted in telling him she had a waiting list, which Cullen knew mostly consisted of single doctors who worked so many hours that they were never home to mess up their homes. Of course, dust fell and spiders spun webs whether or not a person was home.

Angie had found her niche. It was a pretty good gig. The only reason—besides the monetary incentive—she agreed to put in extra hours at Cullen's house to babysit was that he was her original client.

He'd milked that for all it was worth. And then he'd made her an offer she couldn't refuse. Now she was threatening to quit altogether.

Why should he be surprised? Had he ever been able to count on anyone?

"Please, Angie. Stay."

With her purse on her arm, the harried fiftysomething woman sighed and shot him a pained look. The unspoken reality was that the four kids needed to be watched. Like a hawk. They wouldn't sit quietly in front of the television or entertain themselves. In the three days they'd been at Cullen's house, he'd discovered *entertaining themselves* produced foaming blue potions that clogged toilets and stained bathroom floors.

Angie, who had confessed that she didn't like kids, had told him that while she had her eye on one or two of them, the others would be doing something behind her back.

"It's a wonder they haven't burned down the house," she'd said. Until today, Cullen thought she'd been exaggerating.

"You don't have to clean up the mess they made. I'll deal with that. All I'm asking you to do is keep the kids occupied until after I interview Lily Palmer. Play a game with them. One hour at the most and then you can go. I promise."

He wasn't even going to think about what he might do if Lily didn't work out or if she couldn't start today.

Before Angie could answer, Cullen's cell phone rang. He didn't recognize the number. So that meant he had to answer it. Lily might be calling to say she was lost…or to cancel. Maybe he shouldn't answer.

He was already pushing it by leaving the hospital in the middle of the day, asking his colleague Liam Thayer to cover for him. Thayer was the one who had recommended Lily. Cullen prayed to God that she was as perfect for the job as Liam's wife, Kate, had promised.

"Please, Angie." He was relieved when she heaved a resigned sigh and set her purse on the kitchen's granite-topped center island.

"I need to take this call. Just play a game with them. Please. And thank you.

"Cullen Dunlevy," he said as he made his way to his office, where he could still hear the doorbell if the nanny arrived while he was on the phone.

"Hey, Doc, it's Max Cabot. Got a sec?"

Max was the contractor who was building the new pediatric surgical wing at the hospital. The entire Celebration community had rallied to raise money for this much-needed improvement to Celebration Memorial Hospital.

A door slammed in another part of the house. Cullen heard kids shrieking and laughing. Franklin the dog, who had come as a package deal with the kids, barked.

Had they been outside? Wasn't it raining? Judging by the noise level, they were definitely inside now.

"Hold on, Max." Cullen put his hand over the phone. "Hey, guys, can you keep it down, please? I'm on the phone. Play a game with Angie. Play that new Monopoly game we just bought."

His words were lost in the cacophony and the sound of running feet—like a herd of stampeding buffalo. He shook his head.

"Max, I have to call you back, buddy. This is not a good time. I have…a situation here, and I have an appointment that should arrive any minute."

"No problem," said Max. "If you're at home, I'm going to drop by some documents for you to review. I won't stay. It'll just be a drop and run."

Before Cullen could answer, Angie's voice screeched above the kid noise and the barking dog. "Get down! Get off me. You nasty mutt. You stink. Ugggh!" She made a guttural sound like an angry bear. "What is this? What did that dog get on my pants? Get him out of here before I open the front door and put him out myself!"

What the hell?

The dog's bark had changed to a protective growl.

The kids were all talking at once. One of them started crying as Angie continued her nasty-dog tirade.

Cullen put his hand over his free ear as he walked toward the kitchen to make sure Angie and the kids hadn't come to blows. "Good, Max. See you soon. I have to go."

Cullen hung up the phone and hurried into the kitchen.

"What's wrong?" Cullen asked. "Why all the noise?"

Angie had a wet paper towel in her hand and was dabbing at something brown and suspicious on the thigh of her khaki pants. The wet dog, a shaggy black Heinz 57 variety, had taken a protective stance and continued his growl-bark at Angie. Hannah, the youngest of the four kids, was sobbing into her hands. "You can't put him out front. He'll go away just like Mommy did."

The middle girl, Bridget, put her arms around her little sister and hugged her. "Don't worry, Hannah. I won't let her do anything to Franklin."

Angie looked over at Cullen with crazy eyes. "I did not sign up for this." Her hand made a sweeping gesture. "This dog has ruined my new pants with his filth and he's tracked up the floor I mopped. You're going to have to clean that up yourself along with the blue mess, Dr. Dunlevy, because I quit. I'm out of here."

She tossed the wadded paper towel into the garbage, grabbed her purse and speed-walked out of the kitchen toward the front door.

"Good! I'm glad she's gone," said George. He punctuated his declaration with a loud raspberry.

Oh, for the love of all things holy. "Angie, wait, please. Send me a bill for the pants. I'll replace them."

One hand on the door, she paused and looked back. "They cost ninety-five dollars. You can include it in my final paycheck, which you may mail to my house."

Ninety-five dollars? Was she kidding? Who wore expensive pants to clean a house? Of course, with her cushy gig, she didn't have to get her hands—or her pants—very dirty. Angie was all about making the most money expending the least amount of energy.

He and his colleagues were the ones who paid her. Who was the smart one in this scenario?

Angie opened the door and nearly missed running head-on into a perky blonde who stood there smiling, one hand raised as if to knock on the door.

Lily Palmer? Had to be.

One look at her sparkling green eyes and her dimpled smile and Cullen had to fight the urge to hire her right on the spot. She looked like a blonde angel backlit by a ray of sunshine that had finally broken through the gray storm clouds.

As the sound of bickering kids trailed through the half-open front door, he wondered if he could interview her on the front porch and not let her inside until she had taken an irrevocable pledge to work as a nanny for the month of December, which was the length of time she was available to nanny.

God, please don't let the kids run her off the same way they sent Angie packing.

"Hello," she said. Her smile didn't falter and the sparkle in her green eyes didn't fade despite the unwelcoming sounds coming from the house and the figurative horns and fangs that Angie sported as she stood next to Lily on the front-porch step.

"I'm Lily Palmer. I'm looking for Dr. Cullen Dunlevy. I'm here to interview for the nanny position."

"I'm Cullen Dunlevy." That was when he noticed that her eyes weren't just green; they were flecked with gold and her full lips were…stunning. For a fleeting moment he wanted nothing more than to taste those lips, but he mentally shook away the inappropriate thought.

This wasn't a speed-dating interview.

He needed her.

Uh— He needed her to *watch the kids.* He'd be wise to keep himself in check.

Angie laughed. It was a bitter sound.

"I have two pieces of advice for you, Lily Palmer," she said. "Run while you can. Run and save yourself."

Lily looked at the shockingly handsome man who had answered the door and then back at the frazzled-looking middle-aged woman, who made a snorting sound as she turned away from them and virtually jogged toward the driveway.

"Have I come at a bad time?" Lily asked.

She could hear a barking dog and children's voices somewhere behind the half-open front door. The sounds were temporarily eclipsed by the cranking engine of the woman's sports car.

Dr. Dunlevy smiled sheepishly. A dimple winked at her and his hazel eyes shone with boyish charm. Were they hazel or green? She resisted the urge to stare.

"Actually you couldn't have arrived at a better time. I'm sorry about all of this." He held out his hands, palms turned toward the gray sky. "Just so you know, Angie wasn't here applying for the job. Actually she was my housekeeper. Emphasis on the *was*. She just quit. I hope that won't scare you off."

Lily glanced over her shoulder in the direction of where the woman's car had been parked. "Well, no. I teach second graders during the school year. I don't scare that easily. Unless there's something you're not telling me."

If she didn't need this job so badly, she might admit that Angie's exit did concern her just a wee bit. But the private school where Lily taught was closed for the entire month of December—for family ski trips and holiday celebrations. Having a month off was a nice perk for the privileged, but for those who needed money, the unpaid vacation was a hardship.

When she'd heard that Dr. Dunlevy, who worked with the husband of her friend Kate Thayer, was looking for a temporary nanny, it sounded like the perfect job. Especially when she learned he was paying two and a half times what she could earn working a temporary seasonal retail position. She wouldn't let a disgruntled former employee and a barking dog scare her off.

She swallowed her apprehension.

"I guess you really do need extra help," she said.

"You can say that again. Let's go inside. I need to check on the kids. You can meet them, and then we can start over."

Dr. Dunlevy pushed open the door and motioned her inside. He was tall and much younger than she had imagined when Kate had explained the sad situation— that the kids' parents had died in a car accident and the family that was supposed to adopt them had to back out at the last minute. Lily had envisioned Celebration Memorial's chief of staff to be…older and distinguished. But not quite so tall, broad shouldered and good-looking.

She leaned her umbrella against the porch rail and stepped into the foyer. Loosening her scarf, she used the opportunity to take a good look around. Nice place. From the foyer, Lily could see into the living room. It was a bit on the cold and formal side for her taste, but it was nicely done. The high ceilings made the large room, with its stark white walls and modern art, gray marble floors and light-colored leather furniture, look even more expansive. The place definitely had a decorator's touch, and it looked utterly unlived in. It reminded her of the cold, formal feel of a modern museum she'd visited on her senior class trip to New York City. It was interesting to look at, but she couldn't imagine getting comfortable in a place like this. She certainly couldn't imagine young children living here. Not with all this white and glass. It would show every little smidgen of dirt, but it wasn't her place to judge.

Lily caught a movement out of the corner of her eye. When she looked closer, she saw a small girl with dark, curly hair, who couldn't have been any older than four or five, huddled in the corner by the sofa. She had her arms around a big, black wet-looking dog, who sat panting patiently, letting the little girl hug him.

Lily touched Dr. Dunlevy's arm and gestured with a slight nod of her head in the girl's direction.

"That's Hannah," he said and turned his attention to the child. "What are you doing, Hannah? Are you okay?"

The girl didn't answer but seemed to tighten her hold on the dog's neck.

"Hannah, will you come over here, please?" His voice sounded as if he was purposely trying to infuse a smile into it. "There's someone I want you to meet."

The girl gave a quick shake of her head and buried her face in the dog's shaggy back. Dr. Dunlevy looked at Lily and gave an exasperated shrug. He looked exhausted. Lily held up a finger and then walked over to the girl.

"Hi, Hannah, I'm Lily. When I was about your age, I used to have a dog that looked an awful lot like yours. Mine was named Scout. What's your dog's name?"

Hannah remained silent and sullen. Lily sat down on the edge of the couch nearest the girl and the dog. She reached out a hand and let the dog sniff it. He licked her and Lily took that as an invitation to give him a scratch behind the ears.

"You're a good dog, aren't you?" Lily cooed. He was a little smelly, emitting an odor of *eau de wet dog,* but he was definitely a gentle animal.

"His name is Franklin," the girl said in a small, shaky voice. "Will you protect Franklin from Angie? Angie said she was going to put him out in the front yard. She wants him to go away like my mommy did."

Lily's heart tightened. She slanted Cullen a concerned, questioning look. He knit his brow and gave a quick shake of the head.

"Hannah, she didn't mean it," he said. "Angie was just upset because Franklin got mud on her new pants. We're not going to let anything happen to your dog. I promise."

"I don't like Angie." Hannah was crying. "She's mean."

"Oh, honey, please don't cry." Lily took a chance

and reached out and smoothed a dark brown curl off the girl's tearstained cheek. Hannah didn't pull away. "Did you hear what Dr. Dunlevy said? We promise you no one is going to make Franklin go away. If they try, they're going to have to tangle with me."

Lily knew she shouldn't speak for the man who hadn't even hired her yet or talk as if she'd be around to protect the girl. But the poor child was overwrought. She'd lost her parents and her adoptive family, and now she feared she'd have to give up her dog. She must be confused and petrified. With or without permission— or the job—Lily felt it her duty to reassure the little girl.

Franklin licked Lily's hand again.

"Franklin says he likes you," Hannah said, peeking up at Lily through long, thick, wet lashes.

"Well, I like him, too." As Lily smiled at Hannah, she heard young voices coming from the other room.

"The other children are in the family room," said Dr. Dunlevy. "I'd like you to meet them, too."

"Hannah, would you like to come and introduce me to your brothers and sisters?" Lily asked.

The girl shook her head. "I only have *one* brother. One brother and two sisters."

"Thank you for letting me know," Lily said. "I think Franklin needs you now. So Dr. Dunlevy can introduce me to the others. But it was very nice meeting you. I hope to see you again."

Hannah didn't answer. She buried her face in the dog's back. As Lily turned and followed Dr. Dunlevy into the kitchen, she heard the sound of a slamming back door and then stillness settled over the house. The kids must've gone outside.

She could see from the kitchen through to the family room. The far wall was made up of tall windows, but from her vantage point, she couldn't see outside where the kids might have gone.

Since Dr. Dunlevy didn't seem concerned about their whereabouts, she took the opportunity to admire the kitchen. With its stainless-steel appliances and light-colored granite, it had the same sleek, unlived-in feel as the foyer and living room. But then she saw the six-burner gas range and the double oven. She immediately had appliance envy. How many holidays had she and her grandmother talked about the virtues of a kitchen with two ovens? It was a fantasy, like something reserved for television shows featuring dream homes and other places far beyond her reality.

"This is a great kitchen," she said, smoothing her hand over the tiger-eye granite. "Do you cook?"

"Me?" Dr. Dunlevy laughed. "No. Other than using the refrigerator and the espresso machine—" he pointed to a fancy built-in coffeemaker with an array of spouts, nozzles and handles "—I've never used any of the appliances in here."

Lily had to consciously keep herself from sighing. He must've seen the envy in her eyes.

"Do you cook?"

"I do. You might say that food is my favorite hobby."

Standing there with his hands on his hips and his head cocked to one side, he seemed to size her up for a minute. He really was a *good-looking* guy.

"You're more than welcome to cook for me anytime," he said.

The suggestion made her stomach perform an odd dip. She desperately hoped her face didn't betray her.

"I can't remember the last time I had a home-cooked meal."

Ah. Okay.

There it was. It wasn't an invitation to cook for him. Of course it wasn't. Still, for a moment, Lily imagined what it would be like to cook dinner for a handsome man like him in a kitchen like this. Simultaneously, she felt irresistibly drawn to the idea and impossibly out of her element.

"The kids and I have been eating a lot of pizza and takeout since they arrived. Before they got here, I ate most of my meals at the hospital."

She blinked away the ridiculous image of dining with the handsome doctor over a candlelit meal she'd whipped up in this dream kitchen. Good grief, she was his employee. Actually she wasn't even that. He hadn't even offered her the job yet. She needed to remember her place and stay focused on what was important. She couldn't let her mind wander to places it had no business going. So what if he was a handsome man? So what if he had a nice smile and great eyes? If he hired her, her focus would be on the children.

From the kitchen, she followed him into the large family room that looked a little more comfortable than the rest of the house. It had warm wooden floors and an overstuffed sofa arranged across from two masculine-looking leather club chairs. A massive wooden coffee table anchored the grouping. On the wall to her right, a huge flat-screen TV loomed above a fireplace. The windows on the far wall overlooked a nice fenced-in backyard. She could see it better from here and finally caught her first glimpse of the other three kids.

"While Megan, George and Bridget are playing out

back, why don't we talk for a few minutes and then I'll introduce you to them?"

Lily watched the trio running around the yard, playing what looked like a game of tag. At the moment, the kids showed no traces of sadness. Still, her heart broke for them. She hadn't been much older than they looked when her own parents were killed in a car accident. Her one silver lining had been that her maternal grandmother had taken her in and raised her. Her mother had been an only child. So she and her grandmother shared more of a mother-daughter relationship, filling the void for each other the best that they could. At least they'd had each other until she'd died. She'd been gone almost two years now.

Lily had always felt loved and safe and wanted with her. Dr. Dunlevy obviously cared about the well-being of his charges, but she couldn't help wondering what the kids must be going through. To be so young and dependent.

Or maybe the innocence of youth protected them? She hoped so.

Lily settled herself on the edge of the sofa. Dr. Dunlevy sat across from her on the closest chair. With his elbows on the armrests, he steepled his fingers and gazed at her for a moment, as if he were collecting his thoughts.

Finally he said, "Lily Palmer, I'm glad you don't scare easily. Please tell me you know how to make order out of chaos."

She sat up straighter, unsure how to answer that question.

He laughed. "Even if you don't, you come highly recommended."

"That's very nice to know."

She held up a finger. "I have a résumé for you." She slid a folio out of her shoulder bag and retrieved a résumé and list of references. He gave it a once-over.

"Have you had any experience as a nanny in the past?"

"Actually I haven't. No nanny experience per se, but as I said, I'm a second-grade schoolteacher."

"I suppose that's like being a full-time nanny to a bunch of kids," he said.

She nodded. "Pretty much."

"Let's see," he said as he continued to read the rundown of her career history. Suddenly, he put down the paper. "What would you do with four spirited kids? How would you care for them?"

"I would keep them busy, of course. But first you and I would need to discuss your expectations for them."

Cullen nodded and rubbed his temples. "I'm glad you brought that up. I'm not going to lie. They're a handful. They're good kids. Their father was my best friend. But since the loss of their parents, they seem to be working through their grief by acting out. They are the reason my housekeeper quit."

"I'm very sorry for your loss. The loss of your friend, I mean."

Of course he knew what she meant. He wouldn't think she was consoling him over the loss of his housekeeper.

Would he?

Ugh. She felt her cheeks heat. Why was she suddenly so nervous?

Her words hung in the air between them for a few awkward beats.

"Thank you. The kids seem to be resilient, but they have been a challenge. I wanted to be up-front with you about it. It's better that I tell you exactly what to expect than to have you walk out on us like Angie did."

Lily squinted at him. "What do you mean, Dr. Dunlevy?"

"Please call me Cullen. There's no need for formalities."

"Okay. *Cullen*. Did Angie interact with the children?"

"As little as possible. Her main objective was to come in and do her housework. She was my housekeeper for a number of years. With the kids here, it was difficult."

"No disrespect to Angie—I'm sure she's great at what she does," said Lily. "But in my experience, when a child acts up, it's usually a sign that he or she is looking for attention. I would imagine that the kids feel displaced and frightened after losing their parents. I would keep them busy doing fun activities. When kids are busy, they don't have a lot of time to get into trouble. And they tend to sleep better at night because they're tired."

"Would you be willing to get out in the yard and run around with them like that?" He hiked a thumb toward the windows.

"Absolutely. Unless it's too cold or the weather is bad. And then there are lots of things we can do inside, like holiday baking and decorating for Christmas."

She noticed the lack of decorations in his house. It was only December first, and yes, it was still early for some people to decorate. But it had been a tradition in her family to deck the halls the Saturday after Thanksgiving.

"Would you mind if the kids decorated for the holidays?"

"I can't remember the last time I even put up a tree," he said. "I guess the kids will want one since they'll be with me until the New Year, if that long."

"Are they going somewhere after that?"

Cullen raked a hand through his hair and looked a little unsettled. "They're not living with me indefinitely. It just wouldn't be fair to them. That's why I only need a nanny for a month. It may not even be that long if the attorney I'm working with is able to find a family willing to take them in. I want to keep them together. After all they've been through, it wouldn't be right to split them up. Of course, if you agree to take the job and the attorney comes through before the end of the month, I'll pay you through the end of December. That's only fair."

Attorney?

"Those poor kids." The words escaped before Lily could contain them.

Cullen drew in a deep breath and let it out. He seemed to be weighing his words.

Finally he said, "I know it's not ideal, but I'm not married and sometimes I work eighty hours a week. Kids their age need a family to care for them. As much as I hate the thought of shuffling them around, placing them in a good stable environment with a traditional family will be better for them in the long run. The agency is working hard to keep them together, but we're racing against a deadline. They have to go back to school after the first of the year. It would be less disruptive for them to start at their new school than to have them start here and transfer somewhere else."

"They don't have any family who can take them?"

"If they did, we wouldn't be having this conversation."

"Those poor kids have dealt with so much loss at such a young age. To be all alone, except for each other..."

The back door banged open and a cacophony of voices and running feet put an abrupt end to Lily and Cullen's conversation.

Cullen's gaze locked with Lily's. He seemed to be asking, *Are you on board?*

She nodded.

He smiled, then called to the kids, who had blown right past them on their way to the kitchen. "Megan, George, Bridget, please come here. There's someone I want you to meet."

The three of them walked back into the room and stood in front of Lily and Cullen. They cast suspicious, sidelong glances at Lily and then back at each other. Looking more subdued than they had when they were out in the yard, they seemed to be communicating in their own silent language.

Cullen introduced the children. "Please say hello to Ms. Palmer. We've been talking about the possibility of her being your nanny while I'm at work."

"I'm almost eleven years old," said Megan. "I don't need a nanny. I can babysit George, Bridge and Hannah. Mom used to let me do it all the time."

"She did not," cried George. "Don't be a liar."

Megan gave her brother the stink-eye. George clamped his mouth shut and stared at his shoes.

"I'm not lying." Megan sounded a lot older than a typical ten-year-old. Losing both parents made you grow up fast, Lily knew from experience. "I'm just saying, we don't need a babysitter."

"Well, I don't babysit," said Lily. "So I think we're okay. We can just hang out."

"Hang out?" Megan scoffed.

"Yes," said Lily. "Don't you like to hang out?"

Before Megan could answer, the doorbell rang.

"I'll get it," said George. He sprinted out of the room before anyone could protest. Cullen hadn't been joking when he'd said the kids were *spirited*...well, except for Bridget. She hadn't uttered a single word since they'd met.

"Excuse me," said Cullen. "I'm expecting someone. I'm sorry about the interruption. Everything seems to happen at once around here. It's a new way of life."

He smiled and Lily liked the way his eyes creased at the corners. At least he had a sense of humor.

"Continue to talk and get to know each other. I'll be right back."

Lily nodded. It would be good for them to have a few minutes of girl time.

"How old are you, Bridget?" Lily asked.

"She's seven," Megan answered. "George is nine and Hannah, who you haven't met, is five. She's the baby."

"I met Hannah when I first arrived," Lily said. "She was in the living room having some quiet time with Franklin."

"I'm the oldest," Megan underscored.

"And I'll bet you're a very good big sister."

Megan didn't smile, but the compliment seemed to soften her demeanor a bit.

Lily heard Cullen and the voice of another man. Their tones were low and muffled. Whatever they were talking about sounded important. She wasn't trying to eavesdrop, but she was trying to get a sense of how long Cullen might be occupied. He hadn't officially offered her the job and she didn't want to assume it was hers for the taking. He might even have had other candidates to interview.

Still, Lily did her best to engage the kids in conversation, taking care to steer clear of sensitive topics that might upset them. It was more difficult than she'd imagined. That was why she was a bit relieved when George bounded back into the room holding a box of candy. It was one of those big yellow *sampler* types available in drugstores.

Megan shot him another of her stern glares. Maybe she didn't want to share the chocolate. That was fine. Split among four siblings, even the big box wouldn't go far. Lily didn't want to take the kids' candy.

"Since Ms. Palmer is going to be our *babysitter,*" George said, "we should give her something special."

As he held out the box to Lily, Megan crossed her arms and rolled her eyes.

"That's so nice of you, George, but I don't want to take your candy. Save it to share with your sisters."

The boy jumped up and down on one foot. "No! I want to share with *you.* Here!"

He thrust the box at Lily. She took it, fearing he might drop it hopping around like that.

"Okay, just one piece. Thank you—"

When she lifted the lid, something long and black and jumpy sprang out at her. Before Lily could stop herself, she screamed and threw the box into the air.

Chapter Two

An ear-piercing scream eclipsed Max Cabot's explanation of the documents he was dropping off. This time the scream wasn't from one of the girls; it was Lily.

Hell. What had the kids done now? Lily was his only option for a nanny. If they drove her away… He didn't want to put them in day care.

He'd just have to make sure they hadn't scared her off.

"I have to go, Max. I need to go see what's going on in there. I'll look at these and call you later."

When Cullen walked into the kitchen, Lily was on her knees scrambling to pick up what looked like a spilled box of chocolates, shooing the dog away before he could eat them. It looked as though the dog was ahead in the race. The kids stood and watched with guilty-looking faces.

Where had the chocolates come from?

"Everything all right in here?" he asked.

Lily stood up and smoothed her skirt. "Yes. Fine. Everything is fine. Sorry to interrupt you. I dropped the candy that the kids so generously offered to share with me. I shouldn't have screamed. I'm embarrassed."

She screamed over dropping a box of candy?

Cullen squinted at her. He didn't know her well, but she didn't seem like the type to overreact. And when he saw the way the kids were standing there with certain looks on their faces and the way Hannah was looking in from the threshold between the living room and the kitchen, he had a feeling he wasn't hearing the entire story.

"I'm just worried about…the dog," Lily said. "I'm afraid he will get sick from the chocolate. Wouldn't want that to happen. Would we, kids?"

As if on cue, the big, mangy mutt jumped up and put its paws on Lily's stomach and licked her. When Lily stepped back, Cullen saw the dark streak the mutt left on Lily's white blouse. This stain was even worse than the one that had ruined Angie's pants.

Great. Now Lily was going to walk out, and Cullen was out of options except for day care.

"Kids—George, Megan—" He drew a deep breath to take the edge off his voice. "Put the dog on a leash. He has to stop jumping on people. He just got chocolate all over Ms. Palmer."

George took Franklin by the collar and held him while Bridget left the room. Presumably to get the leash.

Lily was brushing at the stain on her blouse.

"I'm sorry about that," he said. "Send me the bill for

the dry cleaning, or if your blouse is ruined, I'll replace it. Sometimes chocolate is hard to remove."

Lily waved him off. "All I have to do is pretreat it and throw it in the washer. It'll be fine. I'm just worried about the dog ingesting all that candy. Isn't chocolate supposed to be bad for them? Should we take him to the vet?"

Ah, hell. She was right.

He pulled out his smartphone. "I have no idea where the closest vet is—"

"It's not chocolate," George murmured as he strained to hold Franklin back. The dog whined in protest. "He doesn't need to go to the vet."

"What was in the box?" Cullen asked.

George looked sheepish. "Mud balls that look like chocolate. They won't make Franklin sick. He eats mud all the time."

There was a beat of silence, during which Megan and Hannah turned and left the room, murmuring something about helping Bridget find the dog's leash.

Cullen counted to ten before he spoke. These pranks were just not acceptable. Sure, the kids were bored and hurting over the loss of their mother. But driving away every single potential caregiver had to stop.

Still, Cullen took extra care to check his tone.

"So, buddy, if they're mud balls, why were you offering them to Ms. Palmer? That's not cool. They could've made her sick."

There was another beat of silence, during which the boy's eyes flashed defiantly before they began to fill with tears, belying his stony expression.

"Oh, no," said Lily. "He wasn't trying to trick me

into eating them. He was just showing me how realistic his candy sculptures were."

She nodded a little too adamantly.

"Candy sculptures?" Cullen asked.

"Yes," Lily said. "As you can see, they're quite true to life."

"Mmm," Cullen answered.

Out of the corner of his eye, he spied another of the mud bombs that had rolled under the table. When he bent to retrieve it, he saw a coiled rubber cobra lying about three feet behind it.

Okay. Now he was starting to piece together the chain of events: the boy handed the lady a candy box; the lady opened said candy box, saw the realistic-looking rubber snake inside, screamed and threw the box.

Obviously it had startled her, but now she was covering for the boy.

Hmm...

Cullen walked around the table and picked up the snake by the tail. It uncoiled and bounded as he held it up. It was so realistic looking that it made Cullen want to wince, but he didn't.

"George, I think this belongs to you," Cullen said. "Did you scare Ms. Palmer with it?"

"Oh, no, he's fine," Lily interjected. "We were just getting to know each other. No harm done. Right, George?"

Seriously?

Cullen looked back and forth between the two of them. Lily was smiling. George looked sullen. Okay. If she wasn't bothered by it, then he wasn't going to press the issue.

Not now, anyway.

In fact, it was nice to see that she had the fortitude to deal with the pranksters. Maybe if they didn't get a reaction out of her they'd stop.

"George, please take the snake and the dog in the other room. I need to talk to Ms. Palmer."

George kept his head down as he yanked the snake out of Cullen's hand and herded Franklin out of the room.

Lily stood there in the middle of the kitchen floor smiling, but looking uncertain and…so damn pretty, even in her stained blouse. Her cheeks were flushed pink. Combined with her green eyes, blond, curly hair and full bottom lip, which she was biting, she looked… Well, the old Van Halen song "Hot for Teacher" came to mind. Cullen forced it out of his head as fast as it had arrived. That was so wrong. Worse than George's pranks and the dog jumping up on her.

He could tell from the short conversation he'd had with her that Lily Palmer was…*different* from the women who usually floated his boat.

She was *different* and she was off-limits…at least until her month of caring for the kids was up.

Stop. Stay on task, he reminded himself.

"You didn't have to defend him," Cullen said. "His behavior was inappropriate."

"He's just a kid," Lily said.

"Does that mean you still want the job?"

Lily blinked at him as if changing channels from champion of children to nanny candidate. "Well, yes. Of course I do."

Cullen exhaled a breath he hadn't realized he'd been holding. Next, he gathered his own inappropriate thoughts and urges, stuffed them into a mental box labeled *Off-limits* and pushed them way in the back of his consciousness. If he was going to hold George to a standard of appropriateness, then he had to set the example.

"Can you start now?"

"Why didn't you get George in trouble?" Megan asked Lily. "Because you totally could've. I'll bet you could've gotten him grounded if you wanted to."

"Nuh-uh," said George. "Uncle Cullen can't ground us. Only Mom and Dad could do that, and they're dead."

Lily winced and brother and sister continued to verbally duke it out. As long as they didn't come to physical blows, she was willing to let them settle it while she regrouped and figured out what they were going to do for the rest of the day.

She hadn't planned on being hired on the spot, much less starting today. If she'd known there'd been a chance of that, she would've planned better. She would've brought things for the kids to do. But, she rationalized, being hired on the spot was far better than having to wait or getting passed over for the job.

She'd had a certain level of confidence coming into the interview since her friends Kate Thayer—who was married to Dr. Liam Thayer, who worked with Cullen at the hospital—and Sydney James, who was good friends with Kate, had both recommended her for the position.

But she had to admit her confidence took a tumble when she saw Angie racing to get out of the house.

Lightweight. She chuckled to herself and then reined it back in. Not everyone was cut out to care for children. Those who weren't had no business trying. There was a fine line between keeping a child in line and breaking his or her spirit.

The Thomas kids needed special care after all they'd been through. Maybe even a bit more slack than she would usually allow the typical kid in her class. To a point.

Through the years, she'd learned that caring for children was not a one-size-fits-all endeavor. It was an ongoing choose-your-battles work in progress.

"How about if we play a game of Monopoly?" Lily suggested with all the enthusiasm she could muster. "Your uncle Cullen said he just got it for you."

Playing a board game, especially one like Monopoly that had the potential to last hours, would not only be a good way to keep them occupied, but might be a good way to get to know them better.

"You know he's not our real uncle," said Megan. "We just call him that. He was my dad's best friend."

"He's a good guy," Lily said. He must've been. It was a commitment to take in four kids. Even if it was just temporary.

"I'm hungry," said Bridget. "Can we have something to eat first?"

Lily glanced at her watch. It was later than she'd realized, well past lunchtime. Cullen had left some money and the number of the local pizza place that delivered. It had been so chaotic she hadn't even thought about whether or not they'd eaten. "You know what? That's a good idea. What kind of pizza should we order?"

The girls wanted cheese. George wanted *the works*. After she placed the order, she instructed the kids to set up the game and count out the money.

While they were busy, she searched the pantry, which housed a full wine refrigerator and not much else. Then she started opening and shutting cabinets in search of a light snack to tide them over. Other than cereal, which they told her they'd had for breakfast, she found a jar of peanut butter in the cupboards and some fruit, baby carrots, a gallon of milk and juice in the refrigerator. That was it for the healthy snacks. Of course, she also found some fancy crackers that were past their expiration date, a jar of olives and a rather smelly, green-looking wedge of blue cheese in the refrigerator.

Typical fare for a bachelor who never ate at home. Then again, he did say he usually ate most of his meals at the hospital.

That was a dismal thought. Unless he had good company.

It was none of her business, but that didn't stop her curiosity. A good-looking guy like that, there was probably a line of eligible women interested in keeping him company as he ate his late-night hospital-cafeteria food. Maybe he even had a girlfriend—though she certainly wouldn't be a very good girlfriend if she wasn't willing to help him out with the kids.

If there was someone, maybe she worked. What else would she do with her time? Maybe she would help him care for the kids in the evening. Because he hadn't said anything about her being a live-in nanny for the month.

Probably because of the girlfriend. What were the chances of a guy like Cullen Dunlevy being unattached? He probably had someone he could count on in the evening.

Beyond the fireworks and breathless delight of a relationship, wasn't one of the best things about being involved knowing you had someone you could depend on? Not in the boring sense of the word, but someone solid. Someone you could count on.

That did sound boring.

Maybe that was her problem. Maybe dependability was just a nice way of saying *boring*. Maybe that was why Josh had broken their engagement.

No, he'd told her she was too fat, that he didn't want to settle for someone who didn't care enough to keep in shape. She was an ample size ten, sometimes spilling over into a twelve. She was curvy and she loved to cook.

To her, food was love. And while she was miles from being thin, she'd never felt fat. She was healthy.

Until the day he'd voiced his repugnance and walked out on her, she'd thought those were the qualities he'd loved about her.

Not so.

Her heart ached at the memory as she grabbed the bag of grapes and carrots and shut the refrigerator door. The kids could snack on them while waiting for the pizza to be delivered.

She'd stop by the store tonight after she got off work and pick up some healthy, kid-friendly food so they wouldn't have to keep ordering in.

They all sat down at the table to start playing the game as they waited for the pizza. Lily asked, "What do you all like to eat?"

"Cookies!" shouted Megan.

"Chicken nuggets," said Bridget.

Hannah tugged on Lily's sleeve and motioned for her to lean closer. Lily did.

"I like mac and cheese," the little girl said.

"Do you?" Lily asked.

Hannah nodded enthusiastically.

"I happen to make the best mac and cheese in the world."

The little girl's eyes grew large. "You do?"

Lily nodded and noticed that the other kids were quietly watching her, except for George. He was fiddling with the game piece shaped like a race car, spinning it on the board, seemingly unaware of the food talk happening at the table.

"I don't suppose anyone would like me to make mac and cheese tomorrow, would they?"

The girls hooted their appreciation. Hannah climbed into Lily's lap and leaned forward to position her game piece, the dog, at the starting square. But George still sat stoically, making the race car spin the way someone might set jacks atwirl.

"What do you like to eat, George?" Lily asked.

The boy didn't answer. Megan nudged him.

"Ms. Palmer wants to know what you like to eat," she said.

The boy shrugged, indicating he wasn't the least bit interested in their conversation.

Lily decided not to push him. "You don't have to call me Ms. Palmer. Why don't you call me Lily?"

Hannah leaned back and looked up at her. "Hi, Lily." She giggled.

"Hi, sweet Hannah," Lily answered.

Hannah giggled again and twirled one of Lily's curls around her finger.

George spun the car so hard that it sailed off the board and skidded across the floor. It disappeared in the space between the wall and the refrigerator.

"Crap!" George growled.

Hannah and Bridget both clasped their hands over their mouths.

"George!" cried Megan. "You're not supposed to say words like that. If Mom were here, you'd be in so much trouble."

"Yeah, well, she's not here anymore." He turned his angry gaze on Lily. "What are you going to do about it, *Lily?*"

It was nearly ten-thirty when Cullen got home that night. After being called away from the office midday, he'd had a lot to catch up on when he got back. Plus, there had been an emergency he'd had to handle. It had taken him that long to get everything in order.

He put his key in the lock, but before he could open the door, someone opened it for him from the inside. Lily was standing there. Cullen's first thought was *What did they do? Please don't tell me you're leaving.*

But Lily simply pressed her finger to her lips in the international sign for *quiet.* She motioned him inside. The door clicked behind him, and for one glorious moment, Cullen stood in the deafening silence. The kids were quiet. The dog wasn't even barking. It was a calm he hadn't heard in days.

Lily walked toward the kitchen and he followed her.

"How in the world did you manage this?" he asked. "Did you slip a tranquilizer into their dinner?"

"No, of course not," she said. "I told you I would tire them out by keeping them busy."

He glanced around at the clean kitchen and the tidy family room, surprised not to see a mess.

"They're angels when they sleep, aren't they?" he said. "This place looks great. Did they help you?"

"A little bit," she said. "We had a good bit of fun, too. In fact, we made Christmas decorations out of some glitter and construction paper I had in my trunk." She gestured toward the table, where he could see several flat and shiny objects neatly laid out.

"But they cleaned up after themselves," she said. "We even tackled that blue mess in the upstairs bathroom."

"The blue potion?" He had forgotten all about it in his rush to get back to work. "You cleaned it up?"

"Potion? Is that what that was?"

She must've had a speck of glitter on her cheek, because something glinted in the kitchen light. Maybe it was pixie dust. Maybe that was her secret. She certainly was as cute as a pixie with her blond hair, laughing green eyes and smooth ivory skin.

"Apparently so," he said. "You didn't have to clean it up."

She chuckled and Cullen had to ball his hands into fists to keep from leaning in and brushing the glitter off her cheek.

"If it sat there any longer," she said, "it was going to either start expanding out into the hall and take over the entire house or dry out on the toilet and tile and stain everything blue. We actually made a game out of it. The kids were great once they got used to the idea that they had to clean up their messes. Are you hungry? Because I'm happy to reheat some pizza for you."

The non sequitur threw him, but as he made the jump from the blue potion to her offer of food, a feeling of gratitude washed over him.

"No, thanks," he said. "I'm sure you're exhausted. You need to get home so you can get some rest for tomorrow."

He wasn't sure that the feeling inside him might not actually be relief. Not only did Lily have the situation firmly under control, but for the first time since the kids had arrived, he was able to take a deep breath and let himself believe that maybe, just maybe, everything was going to work out. And to think there had been a few shaky days there when he'd convinced himself that he'd gotten in way over his head by taking in the kids, even for a little while.

She walked over to the table and picked up her purse. She shrugged into her coat and fished her keys out of her bag before pulling on a pair of red leather gloves. "Actually before I go, I wanted to ask you if you had a schedule you wanted the kids to follow. We didn't really get a chance to talk about specifics before you left to go back to the hospital earlier today."

Schedule? "No. You just keep doing what you're doing. I'll be working late most nights. I won't be around much."

Maybe it was his imagination, but the sparkle in her eyes seemed to dim a few watts.

"There's a park not too far from here. It's just a short drive. You all could go there. I know it's cold outside, but if you bundle them up they'd be fine. Is your car big enough to transport five?"

Lily frowned. "No. I have a sedan. It seats four. I guess that's a problem. Maybe we could walk to the park."

Not unless she was an expert at herding cats.

"I'll call around and see about renting an SUV or

a minivan for you to use. It's too cold outside to walk anywhere, but I know that you can't stay cooped up inside. Let me see what I can come up with."

"That would be great," Lily said. "Hannah was showing me her booster seat today. She's quite proud of it."

Cullen could imagine the girl doing that. For a surreal nanosecond, he saw a flash of what it might be like to keep the kids permanently, with someone like Lily at his side helping him raise them. The thought was simultaneously inviting and terrifying. He blinked it away.

"You'll need a front-door key," he said. "Let me get it for you."

Lily followed him over to a brass key holder that was hanging on the foyer wall just outside the kitchen. He plucked a silver key on a leather key valet.

As he handed it to her, his fingers grazed her soft palm. A tingle of awareness zinged through him and she pulled her hand away a little too fast.

"Feel free to let yourself in," he said. "No need to knock."

She nodded.

"I guess I'll see you tomorrow," she said and turned toward the door. He followed her to lock up after he let her out, feeling a bit like a stray dog trailing along behind a beautiful stranger. She was a good soul who also happened to be a striking woman. A different brand of beautiful that wasn't his usual type. But even if she was, he didn't need to complicate matters by crossing lines that should be clearly drawn.

"Good night," she said.

"Lily?"

She stopped and turned back to face him. The glitter winked at him. Before he knew what he was doing, he reached out and brushed it away. Her cheek was just as soft and smooth as it looked. It took everything he had not to trace his finger along the edge of her jawline and over that full bottom lip—

But then her fingers flew to her cheek.

"It was a speck of glitter," he said. "On your cheek. For a moment, I thought it might be some of that pixie dust you used to work your magic on the kids. But I guess it's just your sparkling personality shining through."

Oh, hell. That was corny.

But she smiled. And blushed. He could even see it in the golden glow of the porch light.

"Thank you," she said. "But I probably have enough loose glitter in my car to decorate the entire neighborhood."

Her keys jingled against the metal of the ring as she gave a little wave of her hand. "See you tomorrow."

He watched her walk away toward her sensible navy blue, four-door sedan and the electricity that had been hanging in the air between them seemed to fade, replaced by the realization that she would be around only until the end of the month.

He felt a little foolish remembering his earlier vision of keeping the kids. She was the one who had set order to the chaos. But she had a job, probably with good benefits, that she would return to after the first of the year. Surely she wasn't interested in being a full-time nanny.

He could ask, but it wasn't likely.

Still, his heart felt heavy when he thought of the

huge task of trying to place all four kids in the same family. The attorney, Cameron Brady, had said he would try, but it was a long shot.

What was he going to do if the perfect family didn't materialize?

It would be impossible to try to care for them on his own; that was just a ridiculous thought that had momentarily run away with his senses. It had been a preposterous lapse of reason. He, of all people, knew that kids need two parents. A mother and a father. Not an absentee pseudo-uncle/father who would spend more time at work than at home. But the fantasy had been fun for the fleeting moment it had lasted.

Chapter Three

At six o'clock the next morning, Cullen was in the kitchen making himself a cup of coffee when Lily showed up at the front door with her arms full of reusable grocery bags.

"Let me help you with those," Cullen said, taking the three sacks from her. "What on earth did you bring?"

"I picked up some things for lunch," she said as she took off her coat and scarf. "And we're going to do some baking today."

As he set the bags on the island in the kitchen, he peered inside and spied grapes, carrots, peanut butter and a loaf of whole-wheat bread, among other things.

"The baking sounds like fun for the kids, but I was going to leave you some money to order pizza again. Wouldn't that be easier than fixing lunch for four?"

"Cullen, most kids love pizza, but not for every meal. I don't mind cooking for them. Really, it's no problem."

Her blond hair hung in soft waves around her shoulders, and her cheeks were still pink from the chilly morning air. She wore a red sweater that looked soft and very touchable and blue jeans that he couldn't help noticing hugged her curves in all the right places.

She was dressed casually and everything about her was appropriate, but how was it that yesterday in the midst of the chaos, he hadn't noticed just *how* attractive she was? How could he have missed that and those curves showcased so nicely this morning?

As he reminded himself that her curves were none of his business, he forced his gaze back to her face. She looked remarkably fresh for having left just eight hours ago. For a split second, it crossed his mind to ask her if she would like to move into the guest room for the month that she'd be watching the kids. But then he thought better of it.

She would probably want a little space and some boundaries during her time off. His gaze dropped to that full lower lip. Or maybe *he* was the one who needed the space. He certainly needed to respect the well-drawn boundaries that should be observed in this type of circumstance.

"Please leave me the receipt for the groceries so I can reimburse you for the things you purchased. Did you go to the store this morning?"

She shook her head.

"Last night," she said and started unpacking the bags, putting things away as if she were completely at home.

He liked her ease and confidence. "You must've gotten home after midnight. Did you get any sleep last night?"

He hadn't.

Even though the house had been quiet and calm, as if everyone had been under Lily's serenity spell, he'd spent a fitful night chasing the squirrels that had raced around his head, making him doubt the realities of taking in four kids—even on a temporary basis. Where had all this doubt come from? Misgivings that had him searching for solutions in the hours when he used to sleep soundly and deeply? Nothing used to disturb him in the few hours he had away from the hospital.

"I'll get used to the new schedule in a few days," she said. "I'm adaptable. But then again, I'll probably just be getting used to the nanny schedule when I have to go back to school. Isn't that how it always works?"

"Then you might as well stay on here rather than go back to school," he said.

She stopped what she was doing.

"Does that mean that you're reconsidering adopting out the kids?"

No. He wasn't. He couldn't. And he had no idea why he'd even suggested she stay on, other than he needed his coffee. "No, I'm still going to find them a home. And I don't mean to make them sound like a litter of animals."

He flinched and started to clarify what he meant. The words were right on the tip of his tongue, but he swallowed them when he heard the sound of the kids moving around upstairs.

"And speaking of," he said.

There was loud stomping and even from a distance it

sounded as though they might be arguing about something. The dog started barking, taking someone's side. Cullen couldn't tell whose. All he knew was that the serenity spell Lily had cast over the house the night before was broken. He hoped to God that she could work her magic again today.

"After they come downstairs, I'm going to say goodmorning and then I need to get to the hospital."

Lily pointed to the coffeemaker. "Don't forget your brew."

"Actually I haven't had time to make it yet. Would you like a cup?"

"If you'll show me how to use that fancy machine, I'll make myself a cup after you get yours," she said. "I don't want you to be late."

They walked over to the coffeemaker. She stood so close that he could smell her perfume, a delicate, feminine floral scent that had him breathing in deeper.

He had just measured the coffee grinds and told her, "You need one scoop for every—" when an ear-piercing scream cut him off and had Lily and him racing into the living room to see what had happened.

Hannah was standing at the top of the steps, crying and holding her finger. Megan was yelling at George, who was holding a stick that should've been in the backyard, not upstairs in the bedrooms.

"You hurt her!" Megan said.

Bridget was standing back quietly observing as her older sister continued to let George have it.

"What's going on up there?" Cullen asked from the bottom of the stairs.

Lily had already gone up to the child and was kneeling at the little girl's side, looking at her finger. "You're bleeding, sweetie. What happened?"

"George took away Franklin's fetch stick. I didn't want him to have it because he said he's going to take Franklin outside without a leash. But I don't want him to because Franklin might run away."

"George, what did you do, buddy?" Cullen asked once he was up there with them.

"He yanked the stick out of her hand," Megan answered. "That's how she got the splinter."

Great. A splinter.

"You have to be careful, pal," he said, trying his best to keep his voice as even as possible. "You're stronger than you realize. I'm sure you didn't mean to do it on purpose, but you hurt your sister. Can you tell her you're sorry?"

All eyes shifted to the boy, whose face had clouded like a thunderhead. "No," he said. "She's dumb. She's a dumb, crying baby."

He turned around and walked out of the room.

Suddenly the dirty dishwater that the hospital tried to pass off as coffee sounded better to Cullen than the strong jolt of joe he usually made for himself, because there was nothing he wanted more right now than to leave all this chaos behind and go to work. Even if the hospital's coffee was bad and that place could be a different brand of bedlam sometimes, at least it came with a chaser of quiet in the form of his closed office door. When he needed to think, all he had to do was shut the door, and unless the place was falling down, no one bothered him. Before they did, they had to go through his administrative assistant, Tracy.

"We need to get this splinter out," Lily said. "Do

you have any tweezers? We'll probably need some hydrogen peroxide and antibiotic ointment. A bandage would help, too."

"It's all in the hall bath," Cullen said. "The room where you cleaned up the blue foam yesterday." The place that always seemed to draw the drama—whether it started or ended there.

Cullen motioned Lily and Hannah to follow him. As the three of them squeezed into the hall bathroom, the dog tried to wedge his way in, too.

Lily scooped up Hannah with one arm and petted Franklin with her free hand, keeping him at bay but allowing him to see that the girl was okay.

"Thank you," Cullen said. Caring for children was infinitely easier with two people. He had no idea how she managed it on her own. Then again, four kids, even kids as spirited as these, must've seemed like a picnic compared to a classroom full. Obviously some people had the gift and others didn't. Lily, he decided as he gathered the supplies, was the child whisperer. He was way out of his league.

He set his cell phone on the counter.

"I'm going to move this over here so it doesn't get splashed," Lily said, pushing it behind her with her free hand.

"Thank you. At the rate my morning's going, I'd probably end up knocking it in the toilet."

He and Lily exchanged smiles, and it was...*nice.* It made him feel as if the day wasn't destined to be all bad.

First he had the little girl wash her hands with soap and water. Then as he prepared to swab Hannah's finger with hydrogen peroxide, she pulled her hand away, tears brimming. "Will that hurt?"

"It shouldn't," Cullen said. "But I'll bet Ms. Palmer will let you squeeze her hand just in case."

"Her name is Lily," Hannah said. "Yesterday, she told us that we could call her Lily."

"Fair enough," Cullen said. He smiled as his gaze snagged Lily's and he wondered why it was that he'd never noticed until now how green her eyes were. And they were flecked with little veins of gold. *Nice.*

"It might be easier for me to get the splinter out if she sits on the counter," he said as he picked Hannah up and set her on the vanity.

He had just started to grab the tiny sliver of wood when his cell phone sounded the arrival of a text.

"That's probably the hospital. I'm late." He nodded in the general direction of the phone, still trying to remove the offending particle. "Would you mind texting them back to say that I'll be right there?"

Lily picked up the phone.

"Oh."

Cullen looked over and met her gaze. "Is there a problem?"

Lily's eyebrows rose and a faint blush colored her cheeks.

"Well, it's not the hospital. It's someone named… Giselle?" Lily cleared her throat. "She says—and I'm paraphrasing here—but she's very eager to see you tonight. It seems she has quite the night planned for you."

Oh, hell.

Heat warmed his face. He glanced down at Hannah to see if she'd caught on to the situation. But she was studying the finger that was now splinter free.

"Here—never mind." Cullen held out his hand for the phone. After Lily gave it to him, he shoved it into his pants pocket as if the action could undo Lily having read the message, which was bound to be graphic, knowing Giselle.

He felt like a letch for having subjected her to it. Of course, if he'd known Giselle would pick that precise moment to offer a preview of coming attractions, he wouldn't have asked Lily to pick up the text. In fact, he'd been so busy since the kids arrived that he'd completely forgotten he was supposed to see her.

Was that tonight?

He couldn't bring a woman like her around while Lily and the kids were here. Before he'd taken the kids into his home, he hadn't realized all the ways they might change his life. When had he ever recoiled from a spicy Giselle text or passed up a chance to see her? But given the circumstances, he didn't have a choice but to decline.

"Does your finger feel better, Hannah?" he asked after he'd slathered it with antibiotic ointment and applied a bandage.

She nodded through a one-shoulder shrug. "Sort of. It would feel much better if I had a princess bandage."

Lily took the little girl down from the vanity, held her good hand and led her out of the bathroom without looking at Cullen. "The next time I go to the store, I'll make sure to get some princess bandages. A princess should always have a special bandage. You're very brave to wear the ordinary one for now."

Cullen stood alone for a moment, listening as their conversation grew faint. He certainly hadn't thought taking in the kids would throw him into a crisis of conscience. After all, he was single. He and the women he dated were consenting adults and very clear about the no-strings-attached nature of their relationships. He wasn't doing anything wrong.

So why did it feel as though he was?

He took a deep breath and reminded himself that it wouldn't be this way forever. The kids would be living with him only until the end of December. Then he could resume life as he knew it.

Nothing said *let's be friends* like a big stack of homemade pancakes. After Cullen made his awkward exit, Lily did her best to put the racy contents of the text she wished she'd never read out of her mind.

It wasn't easy to erase the image of Cullen doing the things Giselle had so graphically described in her message. The only problem was her brain kept imagining Cullen doing those things to *her*.

Lily wasn't a prude—she'd been engaged and had enjoyed a healthy relationship with her fiancé before everything turned south—but those thoughts were so inappropriate when she was supposed to have her mind on the kids. For God's sake, the thoughts were inappropriate even if she wasn't watching the kids. Cullen Dunlevy was her boss. And even as progressive and open-minded as she fancied herself, she certainly was no Giselle.

She forced the thoughts out of her mind—or at least relegated them to the very back, dark corners of her overactive imagination—and fired up the griddle she'd brought with her. She made cheerful small talk with the kids as she mixed up a batch of pancake batter for them.

She let them flip their own, which the girls loved.

George, however, was less than impressed. He slumped on a bar stool at the kitchen island, kept his head down and his attention on his handheld video game while the three girls enjoyed their breakfast and chatted among themselves.

"Come on, George. Will you please put down the game for five minutes so you can make your pancakes?" Lily cajoled. "It'll be fun."

George didn't answer.

"Just five minutes, George, please? That's all it will take."

Nothing.

"I'll make a deal with you," Lily said. "If you'll make your pancakes, I'll let you lick the bowl when we make sugar cookies after breakfast."

George looked up, his eyes glossy with irritation. "Doesn't Uncle Cullen pay *you* to make my breakfast?"

Lily's eyes widened at the boy's cheeky response. She walked around to the same side of the island where George was sitting, pulled out the bar stool next to him and sat down.

"Your uncle Cullen pays me to look after you." She took care to keep her voice even and soft. She was used to dealing with the occasional conflict like this in the classroom, but George's attitude grew from a place of hurt. The boy probably felt angry and displaced after losing his parents and the adoptive parents who had agreed to take in his sisters and him. He was in limbo and unsure where they would end up, much less if he and his sisters would be able to stay together. Of course, Cullen said keeping the kids together was his goal, but Lily couldn't help wondering how realistic it was, especially given that he was intent on finding them a place by the end of the year.

The boy had returned his attention to his video game, his thumbs stabbing angrily at the buttons on the device. What George needed more than a battle of wills over pancakes was some compassion and understanding.

Lily stood. "Okay, if you don't want pancakes for breakfast, you can have milk and cereal. Help yourself."

George didn't respond. He simply poured himself a bowl of oat cereal, skipping the milk. He took his breakfast and his game and headed into the other room.

"George, don't you want to help bake cookies?" Lily asked, giving it one more try.

George turned around and glared at her. "No." He started to walk away.

"Then what would you like to do?" Lily asked. "I don't think your uncle Cullen wants you spending your entire Christmas break playing video games."

He leveled her with a blank stare.

"I could get you some books if you'd like to read."

He grabbed a handful of cereal and shoved it into his mouth.

"Or if you don't want to read, tell me some of the things that you enjoy doing—besides video games."

"Not baking," he said. "Baking is for girls."

She thought about telling him that some men were pastry chefs and they were actually quite famous for it, but she knew there was no sense in trying to win him over.

"On the radio this morning, I heard about a boys' basketball camp that's going on during the holidays over at the community center," Lily said. "Would that interest you?"

His expression changed. It wasn't quite what you'd call *agreeable,* but it was a far cry from the defiant make-me face he'd worn just a minute ago.

"If you'd like, I can talk to your uncle Cullen about getting you signed up for it."

He nodded, then turned and disappeared into the next room with his cereal and game.

When the girls were finished with their breakfast, Lily put Hannah and Bridget to work measuring flour into large bowls. She had Megan creaming butter and sugar together. Her plan for the day was to have the kids make and decorate Christmas sugar cookies. She also wanted to teach them how to make a Christmas bread called *stollen,* a confection filled with dried fruits and marzipan.

"A long time ago, in Germany," she said, "they used to make a huge loaf of special Christmas bread called *stollen.* It had all kinds of fruits and spices and a special filling. It weighed tons and it was big enough to share with everyone in the city. They'd bring it out and feed everyone."

Megan was squinting at her. "They ate stolen bread? Who did they steal it from?"

"No, it wasn't *stolen,* as in illegally taken from someone," Lily said. "It's called *stollen.* It sounds the same, but it's completely legal. Believe me, I wouldn't teach you about anything illegal."

"How big was it?" Megan asked, still looking as if she wasn't buying the story.

"What?" Lily asked.

"You said the stollen bread loaf was big enough to

feed the entire city," she said incredulously. "How big is that?"

"This big?" Hannah hopped off the bar stool and held out her arms wide.

"Oh, much bigger than that," Lily said, winking and playfully waving her off.

"*This* big?" Hannah's arms were stretched so wide she was bending backward.

"Yes, maybe that big," Lily said. "Possibly. But maybe even a little bit bigger."

She reached down and tickled the little girl. Hannah squealed in delight.

"I've never seen the big loaf of bread in person," Lily said. "But I've heard it was so big they had to put it on a horse-drawn carriage and pull it around. I mean, if it was big enough to feed the *entire town,* it had to be huge."

All three girls gasped.

"Several years ago, they revived the stollen festival in Germany. Now it's called Stollenfest. Every year at Christmastime, they still bake a gigantic loaf all yummy and covered with powdered sugar. They still put it on a big carriage and parade it through the streets on the way to the Christmas market. When they get there, they cut it into lots of pieces with a huge knife. I mean, think about it. You'd need a gigantic knife to cut a loaf of bread that big, don't you think?"

The girls nodded.

"Well, they cut it up, but now instead of giving it away, they sell it and give the money they make to a charity that helps people."

Megan nodded as if she believed Lily.

"When do they do that?" asked Hannah.

"Stollenfest takes place in the middle of Advent."

"What's Advent?" Bridget asked.

"It's the period of time leading up to Christmas. Usually the three or four weeks before. So Stollenfest probably takes place two weeks or so before Christmas. So they're probably getting ready for it right about now. It's a very fun day."

"Oh, my gosh," said Hannah, dramatically putting her hand on her forehead. "That's still a long time before Christmas comes. That's like *forever*."

Lily smiled. To a kid, the weeks before Christmas did seem to last forever. "Well, in Dresden, Germany, that's how they make the time before Christmas go faster. They do lots and lots of baking. So that's what I thought we could do."

The girls were watching her attentively.

"So, what do you say?" she asked. "Do you want to learn how to make stollen? We could have our own Stollenfest right here in Celebration."

"Are we going to make one big enough to feed the entire town?" Hannah asked, jumping up and down. "Are we going to parade it through the streets?"

"Well, no," Lily said. "We don't have an oven that big. But we can make smaller loaves from my great-grandmother's recipe. Maybe we could make enough to give it to the neighbors as Christmas presents?"

The girls clapped their hands and nodded their agreement.

"Can we make some for Uncle Cullen, too?" Bridget asked.

"You bet we can. It's a lot of fun to make. My grandmother and I used to always bake it during the holidays. I think out of everything, stollen puts me in the best Christmas spirit."

"Why doesn't your grandmother come and make it with us?" asked Bridget.

Lily considered her answer for a moment, afraid that bringing up the subject of death might upset the kids. Tiptoeing around the truth would be worse. If it upset them she could help them learn to cope.

"My grandmother isn't living anymore," she said.

"Is she with the angels?" asked Hannah, her eyes earnest and sober as she got back on her stool.

"Yes, she is," said Lily.

"My mommy and daddy are with the angels, too," Hannah said.

"Hannah…" Megan's tone was a little sharp, but the sadness in her eyes reflected her grief.

"It's okay to talk about your parents, Megan," Lily said. "When you're ready."

The girl looked back down at her bowl and stirred its contents halfheartedly.

"I understand how hard it is," Lily said. "My parents are with the angels, too."

All three girls looked up at Lily.

"So you're just like us?" said Bridget. "Maybe that's why I like you so much."

Hannah got down off her stool again and came over and hugged Lily. "I like you, too," the little girl said, looking up at her with heartbreaking blue eyes.

Emotion caught in Lily's throat and she had to swallow hard to contain it. She smoothed a wayward dark curl off Hannah's forehead.

"We need to stick together, don't we?" Lily said.

Bridget and Hannah nodded. Megan stared at her,

but now there was something softer in her expression. Lily knew not to push it, but all the signs were an indication that the girl would come around soon enough.

"Megan, do you know how to knead bread?" Lily asked.

The girl shook her head.

"That's what you have to do to bread dough to make it good," Lily said. "Would you like to learn? I'll bet you'd be a good baker."

The girl's slight smile warmed Lily's heart. After she got Bridget and Hannah set up to roll out the sugar cookies, she helped Megan mix the ingredients for the stollen.

"Don't you think we need to have a Christmas tree if we're going to have a Stollenfest?" Megan asked. "Do you think Uncle Cullen will get one?"

"I don't know," Lily said. "I can't imagine why he wouldn't, but we can ask him."

After the words escaped, she wanted to take them back. Cullen wasn't a traditional man. He could very well have no plans to get a tree. Sure, it was early in the month, but there was no evidence that he even intended to put up any Christmas decorations.

Decorating for the holidays had been a beloved tradition in Lily's family. They'd always gotten their tree the Saturday after Thanksgiving and had it brimming with tinsel, ornaments and garland before they ushered in the month of December. Now here they were, well into the first week of the month, and they had some work to do if they were going to get this house in Christmas shape.

George sauntered into the room. Lily was happy when he seemed to take an interest in the dough that she and the girls were shaping into oblong loaves. When he started to poke at the dough, she had him wash his hands, which he did without any back talk.

He was coming around easier than Lily had expected. Her heart warmed and she thought it must be because of the basketball camp.

Score one for me. But George would be the real winner in the end, and that was all that mattered.

After he dried his hands, he went back to his place beside his older sister, where Lily had set out some bread dough for him.

"Lily, will you come over here and sit next to me and show me how to do this?" he asked.

"Of course, George. I'd love to."

He really could be a sweet boy. She couldn't believe that she had gotten through to him so easily. Then again, kids were resilient. Probably more so than adults.

As she pulled out the bar stool to sit down, Megan shrieked.

"Don't sit there!"

Lily flinched, taken aback by the girl's abrupt demand. She took in a deep breath and mentally counted to ten to steady herself. They would have to set some guidelines on what was appropriate and what wasn't, but she didn't want to overreact. Maybe she'd talk to Cullen and get him to help her out so the kids understood that she and Cullen were united when it came to expectations.

The image of Cullen with a bare muscled chest and strong arms that closed around her scurried to the forefront of her mind before she could preempt it. She blinked the image away.

"George, do not prank Lily," Megan demanded. "He

wanted you to sit on the whoopee cushion and then he was going to make fun of you for…" Megan made a face. "You know…." She reached over and put her hand down hard on the whoopee cushion so that it made its characteristic sound.

The little girls shot scathing looks at George.

"That's not funny, George," said Bridget. "Don't mess with Lily. We like her. She's nice."

"Yes, we do," said Hannah.

All right, so George had had ulterior motives. It was just a prank. It wouldn't hurt anyone and Lily would've laughed right along with George if she had fallen into his snare. But she couldn't help being touched by the way the girls had stood up for her. Apparently pranking was serious business and only executed on those who deserved to suffer—physically or emotionally.

The boy's face turned bright red.

"Say you're sorry," said Megan, in full big-sister mode.

George puffed up, as if his sisters taking Lily's side was the ultimate betrayal.

"Say it!" Megan stood up. Even though George was taller than his older sister, the girl still seemed to hold the authority.

"I'm sorry." George's words were barely audible, but Lily was amazed that he complied.

"No harm done," Lily said, smiling at the boy. "Why don't we put the first batch of sugar cookies in the oven? It won't take them very long to bake. I think we all need a cookie and milk break."

The boy lifted his head and looked Lily in the eye, and for the first time she saw past his petulance and bravado and glimpsed the scared little boy. It dawned

on her that his pranks were a way of driving away people before they could leave him. She wanted to reach
out and hug him, but she knew better. That would only
embarrass him.

The best thing she could do would be to show him
that he had a steadfast friend in her. She wasn't going
anywhere. Though she might not have control over
where the kids ended up, she certainly could make sure
they felt safe and wanted while they were in her care.

Chapter Four

Cullen got home shortly after seven, early by his standards. When he walked through the front door, he was welcomed by the sweet aroma of heaven. Something smelled delicious. His stomach growled its appreciation.

It had been a long day at the hospital. The egg sandwich he'd grabbed in the cafeteria on his way to his office held him for a while, but he hadn't had time to stop for lunch.

He was ravenous. Whatever Lily was cooking smelled exactly like what he needed.

The sound of running water, clanking dishes and Christmas music emanated from the kitchen. As he took off his coat and turned in that direction, something white and sparkly in the living room window caught his eye.

Apparently the kids had made paper snowflakes. Upon closer inspection, he discovered they'd covered them with silver and white glitter before stringing them on a piece of twine and placing them in the window that overlooked the backyard.

He remembered the fleck of glitter that he'd brushed off Lily's cheek last night and the softness of her skin.

He wanted to touch her again.

He gave himself a mental shake and forced the thought from his mind.

Instead, he focused on how they'd swagged the same window that housed the snowflakes with a cranberry and popcorn garland. There was a small wreath on the wall above the couch, made from dozens of kid-sized hands traced and cut out of green construction paper and attached to something round so that it resembled a holly wreath.

The homemade decorations were a sharp contrast to the room's modern furnishings, but they added a homey touch that was…nice. At least they added warmth and festivity to the room. It took him back to when he was growing up. His mom had worked two jobs to keep food on the table and a roof over their heads. There was no extra money for trees and fancy decorations. One year his mom had gotten creative and they'd done little projects like this. But in subsequent years, she'd been too busy working to make decorations again. Even though that one Christmas had been nice, memories of it made him realize what he was missing out on; it made him think that sometimes it was better to go without than to have a little taste of something you could never have.

Now Cullen never bothered to decorate for Christmas. What was the point when it was just him and he spent most of his waking hours at the hospital? The nurses and staff always put up a tree and hung small stockings with everyone's names on them. That was enough.

But it was different for kids.

He ran his hand over the green paper wreath one more time. But sounds from the kitchen pulled him back to the present, reminding him that was where he'd been headed originally. His stomach growled again, seconding the motion.

As he approached the kitchen, the music changed to "Jingle Bell Rock." He'd opened his mouth to say hello, but Lily, who was washing dishes, started singing along and moving in time to the music in a little dance that made his pulse kick up as he paused in the doorway to watch her.

The corners of his mouth quirked.

The way she moved wasn't suggestive or blatantly sexy, and because it wasn't, it was all the sexier. It was the way she moved with such unselfconscious abandon that made his heart ache. And for a moment he lost himself in her grace.

As if she sensed him there, Lily's head snapped in his direction. She froze and her cheeks flushed a pretty shade of pink.

Her hand fluttered to her throat. "Oh! I didn't realize you were home. I thought you had a date tonight."

The side of Cullen's mouth twisted up. "What? And miss tonight's performance? Never."

She covered her face with her hands and shook her head. "Just pretend you didn't see that."

"I'd pay to see that." He walked into the kitchen

and propped his hip against the counter next to the sink. "You have a nice voice. Don't stop on my account. Please."

"You weren't even supposed to be home. What happened to Giselle? It sounded like she had a fun night in store for you."

His smile faded. "Yeah, about that. I'm sorry you had to see the text. It was inappropriate and I wanted you to know I would never have purposely subjected you to it."

Her cheeks flushed again and she waved him off. "Don't worry about it. It just sounded like Giselle had big plans for you. What happened?"

"Giselle tends to make a lot of big plans," he said.

"And that's a problem?"

He opened his mouth to explain that when any woman started to get too close it did become a problem, but as he looked into her large green eyes, he wisely thought better of it.

"I think while the kids are here, Giselle and I are going to take a break."

"I see," she said.

He could see the wheels turning. So before she had a chance to ask any more questions, he changed the subject. "Speaking of… Where are the kids?"

"They're upstairs watching a movie. Are you hungry?"

"Famished. What smells so good?"

"It's just a simple beef stew. If I'd known you'd be home for dinner, I would've made something nicer."

"Are you kidding? Beef stew sounds perfect on a night like this. The temperature has really dropped.

In fact, the weather forecasters are saying it's going to freeze tonight."

"Sit down." Lily motioned to the island. "I'll dish you up a bowl of stew and warm you up."

Cullen lowered his body onto a stool. "How was your day? Did you and the kids get along okay?"

"We had a great day," Lily said.

"How was George? He didn't give you any trouble, did he? No more snakes in chocolate boxes?"

"He's a good kid," she said as she took a bowl down from the cabinet. "Has a will of iron, but still, I know he doesn't mean any harm."

Cullen narrowed his eyes. "Sounds like something happened today?"

Lily set the bowl of steaming stew and a plate containing several pieces of bread in front of him, and then she produced a spoon and napkin, which she set alongside the bowl.

"No, not really," Lily said. "Nothing I can't handle. He didn't want to bake with his sisters and me. He informed me that baking was for girls."

Cullen grimaced.

Lily nudged a plate that was full of colorfully decorated sugar cookies toward him. It was clear that she had given the kids free rein when it came time to decorate them. Some of the cookies were more *artfully* garnished than others.

"You must have the patience of a saint." He smiled up at her as he unfolded his napkin and draped it over his left leg.

"I don't know about that."

"Aren't you going to join me?"

"No, but thank you," she said. "I ate with the kids,

but I'm happy to keep you company. Unless you want some peace and quiet?"

"Please stay," Cullen said.

Lily nodded and slid onto the stool next to Cullen. "How would you feel about George participating in a basketball camp? There's one at the community center over the holiday break and I think it would be good for him. It would let him burn off some of his excess energy. It would get him out of the house away from his video games. I'll take him and pick him up."

Cullen chewed his bite and swallowed. "This stew is delicious. I think basketball camp is a great idea. Let me know how much it costs and I'll leave a check so you can get him registered."

They sat in companionable silence while Cullen spooned up a few more bites.

"Did he help with the decorations you put up in the living room? I think they're a lot of fun. They really make the house festive."

"He did," Lily said. "A little bit, anyway. But speaking of being festive… The kids were asking whether you were going to get a tree. No pressure. I just promised them I'd ask. If you'd rather not go to the trouble, I could bring in a little tabletop tree I have at home."

A tree? Of course the kids would want a tree. Why hadn't he thought about that before now?

"I think that's a great idea." Cullen glanced at his watch. "In fact, it's only seven-thirty. Why don't we see if the kids want to go pick out one tonight? Would you come with us?"

Lily hadn't planned on being included in the tree shopping. Or maybe it was more apt to say she hadn't planned on Cullen taking an interest in it. In fact, she had been thoroughly surprised to look up and see him home so early, standing there in the doorway, watching her.

She'd been mortified that he'd caught her singing along to "Jingle Bell Rock" like a fool. But she had to admit that she'd loved the way he'd been looking at her. There was something in his eyes that was like a soft caress…something in the way all his attention seemed to be trained on her. For a glorious second, she reveled in it, but then the embarrassment set in and that had been the end of that.

Now here they were, piled into the SUV that Cullen had rented for the month that she'd be watching the kids. They probably looked like a family to anyone who didn't know better. Even if it wasn't true, it was fun to pretend.

When they got to the tree lot, the kids tumbled out and took off running into the tens of dozens of Christmas trees.

"Stay together," Lily called after them. "And don't go too far. Stay where you can hear us call for you."

The temperature had dropped. Lily turned up her coat collar to fend off the chill breeze.

"Are you cold?" Cullen asked.

"I'm fine," she said as the two of them walked side by side under the golden glow of the small globe lights strung over the forest of firs, pines and spruces.

For a foolish moment, Lily wondered what it would be like to be nestled in the warm crook of Cullen's arm or, better yet, safe and warm in his embrace. With arms like his, it was the best place she could imagine on a night like this. But the sound of the children laughing snapped her out of it and landed her firmly in cold reality.

Those were the same arms that held Giselle, she reminded herself, just in case there was any temptation to continue the ridiculous fantasy.

Why had he changed his mind about seeing Giselle tonight? She hadn't expected him to come home so early. She certainly hadn't planned on him eating dinner at home—especially after he'd told her not to count on him and to go ahead and feed the kids. She was suddenly glad that she'd had the foresight to make extra stew. Granted, she'd planned on asking him if he wanted to take it with him for lunch tomorrow.

It was even better that he'd been home to enjoy it fresh and hot off the stove…and far away from Giselle, sender of naughty texts and instigator of mental pictures that she hadn't been able to get out of her head all day.

Like right now.

She tried to blink away the image of a bare-chested Cullen before her mind's eye could meander to places it had no business going. But it was an exercise in futility; telling herself not to think of something simply made her mind zero in on the thought.

The only solution was to distract herself.

"This is a pretty tree." She pointed to an eight-foot blue spruce and then realized that it would be dwarfed under the high ceilings in Cullen's house. "Maybe something like this, only taller?"

Then again, maybe a smaller tree would better serve the kids, since they'd be the ones decorating it. At least she suspected they would since Cullen said he'd likely not be home most evenings…yet here he was with them to-

night…instead of spending the night naked with Giselle…
and just what would he look like naked—?

Stop it!

"That one does look good," Cullen said, considering the tree she'd pointed out. He was holding it up and
rotating it slowly.

She nodded, suddenly at a loss for anything to say.

When was the last time a man had rendered her
tongue-tied?

But Cullen Dunlevy, with his easy charm and disarming smile, made her as shy as a schoolgirl walking with her crush.

And that was precisely the problem. She wasn't a
schoolgirl and he wasn't her crush. He was her boss.
She needed the job and the kids needed a nanny. It was
so inappropriate to even think about mixing business
and pleasure—or what he'd look like naked.

Stop it!

"May I ask you a personal question?" he asked.

Her breath caught. Personal? That certainly didn't
sound like small talk about the tree or the weather.

"Sure," she said.

"Why aren't you married with kids of your own?"

She felt herself flinch.

He must've noticed, because he turned his attention
back to the tree and said, "You just seem like the kind
of woman who'd be married with a family of her own.
Like someone would've snapped you up by now. Now
that I've said that out loud, it sounds way too personal.
I'm sorry. Pretend I didn't ask."

"No, I don't mind."

Well, she did. Sort of. It wasn't exactly her favorite
subject to talk about, but she'd wanted a *real* conver-

sation and this was their first one of substance. She wasn't about to go back to shallow.

"Honestly, I thought I'd be married by now. I should've been. I was engaged. I was supposed to get married last fall, but it didn't work out."

"I'm sorry," he said. "But if you want to know the truth if it wasn't going to work out, it's better you found out sooner rather than later."

"Do we speak from experience?"

"Yes, I do. I was married once and it didn't work out. Divorce is hard. When the relationship isn't right, someone always gets hurt."

"Was that someone you?"

The answer was written all over his face.

It was her turn to say, "Now *I'm* getting too personal. You don't have to answer that."

He smiled, but she saw the sadness in his eyes. "You were forthright with me—"

"Hey, Uncle Cullen and Lily, come here."

Lily looked up and saw Bridget motioning them toward a cluster of Fraser firs. "I want to show you something."

"Lucky you," she said. "Saved by the kiddo. You're off the hook for now. But this conversation is to be continued."

He gave her a warmer smile this time as he returned the tree back to the display. "Somehow I know you're going to hold me to that, aren't you?"

"Of course I will."

She and Cullen joined Bridget, who was with Megan, who had appeared from behind one of the trees.

"Uncle Cullen, what is this down here?" The older girl pointed to something under the tree.

Hannah clasped both hands over her mouth, but the gesture didn't contain her giggle.

What were they up to? *Something* was going on.

"I don't see what you're talking about," said Cullen.

"Lily, you see it, don't you?" The girl pointed and scowled seriously as if the unknown object was very important. "Here, look closer."

The girl crouched down and pointed under the tree.

Lily and Cullen exchanged bemused glances, and together they bent down to see if they could get a better look at whatever it was that had the kids so perplexed.

Suddenly they heard a thud behind them. George had appeared from somewhere and was holding a small green branch over their heads.

"Kiss her! Kiss her! Kiss her!" Hannah sang as she jumped up and down.

"It's mistletoe," Bridget exclaimed.

"Now you have to kiss," Megan said smugly. "If you don't, it's like you'll be breaking the rules of Christmas."

For one breathtaking moment, Lily's gaze locked with Cullen's and time stood still.

Something flickered in his eyes.

He was going to kiss her.

She wanted him to kiss her.

But the sound of a ringing cell phone broke the spell. Lily flinched and pulled back, mortified by what she'd almost let happen.

"You'd better answer that," she said.

It might be Giselle.

Women like that always had impeccable timing.

Before Cullen pushed the button to pick up the call, he leaned in and dusted her lips with a featherlight kiss.

"We don't want to break the rules of Christmas, do we?"

Chapter Five

It was one of those days.

No, it was worse. Lily had never had a day when quite so many things had gone wrong. Cullen had been distant when she got to work that morning. Or maybe she'd been the distant one. The kiss, even as chaste as it was, had left them in an awkward place.

After he kissed her, he'd walked away to take his call. Lily had stayed with the kids, distracting them from their whooping and hollering delight over their successful prank. She'd reminded herself that was all the kiss had been: the product of a prank.

A prank that had suddenly made everything awkward.

And that had set the tone for the day. After Cullen had nearly fallen all over himself to get out the door to work, Lily loaded the kids into the rented SUV and drove George to the community center to get him signed up for the basketball camp. He'd already missed three days of it. So she'd wanted to get him there as soon as possible.

How was she supposed to know that he needed a specific kind of shoe to play basketball? A shoe with non-marking soles. Apparently shoes with dark soles scuffed up the court. They should've included this tidbit in the registration information.

The coach had been nice about it, but he'd also been adamant that George could not play until he had the proper shoes. He'd even told Lily where she could buy them—at Main Street Sporting Goods right there in downtown Celebration.

That sounded easy enough.

Main Street Sporting Goods was five minutes away from the community center. They could go get the shoes and have him back within a half hour, maybe even before the kids had finished the warm-up drill if they hustled.

Well, she could've gotten him back in time if Main Street Sporting Goods had had George's size in any of the shoes the coach had recommended.

They didn't.

Apparently lots of other little boys needed shoes with non-marking soles, too, because the store was sold out. The sales associate was good enough to call the national chain sporting-goods store in Dallas, which was about twenty minutes away. What choice did Lily have but to load the kids back into the car and head to Dallas? If they didn't dawdle, they could be back before lunch, right?

Well, they could've been if she hadn't been in such

a blasted hurry that she'd neglected to check the gas gauge and realized that it was frightfully low...until she and the kids ran out of gas halfway between Celebration and Dallas.

How could she have been so stupid? Wasn't that one of the things that her grandmother had drilled into her head when she taught Lily to drive?

Always check your gas gauge before you back out of the driveway.

Besides, rental cars usually came with only a minimal amount of gas. After the SUV had been delivered late yesterday afternoon, they'd driven to the tree lot. Granted, it wasn't a long haul, but after the electricity of that kiss, stopping for gas had been the furthest thing from either of their minds. Case in point of why she didn't need to distract herself with an inappropriate crush on a man she had no business thinking inappropriate thoughts about.

She was driving her own car back and forth between home and Cullen's house, driving the SUV only when she needed to take the kids somewhere. Even if she could've chalked it up to distraction, thanks to her carelessness, here she was, stuck along the side of the road with the children she'd been charged with looking after.

"I want to go home, Lily," Hannah whined.

"We can't go home until we get my shoes," said George.

"Why are we stopped?" Bridget asked.

"We're out of gas," Lily said matter-of-factly. She tried to keep her voice calm and even because the kids would follow her lead. Even though panic and frustration were clawing at the back of her throat, she wasn't going to lose it in front of her charges. Running out of gas was humiliating. But that didn't mean she was entitled to lose her cool in front of them.

"Out of gas?" Megan asked, an incredulous edge to her voice. "What are we supposed to do now?"

That was a good question. She searched in the glove box to see if the rental came with any sort of roadside assistance. She'd read somewhere that it was an extra that you had to purchase at the time of the rental. Cullen hadn't mentioned it and she couldn't find any indication in the paperwork that he'd opted in.

Fishing her phone out of her purse, Lily curved her lips into the most sincere smile she could muster. "I'm going to call someone to come and help us."

"Uncle Cullen?" asked Bridget.

Heavens no.

"Uncle Cullen is so busy," Lily said. "I don't want to bother him. I'm going to call a friend of mine who doesn't live too far from here."

First, she tried to call the rental company, but they wouldn't talk to her because she couldn't supply the credit card used to rent the car.

Darn it.

Next, she looked up Sydney James's number in her contacts and hit the call button. The phone rang and rang…three times…four times…before Sydney's proper, crisp voice sounded on her voice-mail recording.

"Hello, you've reached Sydney. Please leave a message and telephone number after the tone and I'll call you back at the earliest opportunity."

The earliest opportunity might mean that afternoon, especially if Sydney was on location shooting a segment for *Catering to Dallas,* a reality TV show that

chronicled the inner workings of the Celebrations Inc.
Catering Company.

That was how Lily had met Sydney. The show wanted
to give a local couple the wedding of their dreams. The
only catch was that the wedding and the days leading
up to the ceremony and reception would be filmed for
Catering to Dallas and aired on national television.

Lily won the contest. She, who had never won anything in her entire life, had been named Celebration's
Bride. Little did she know the honor would also lead
to the ultimate demise of her long-term relationship
and near broadcast of her humiliation.

She and her boyfriend, Josh Stockett, had been dating for years. They'd talked about getting married…
or, if truth be told, *Lily* had talked about getting married. They'd been together forever. She loved him. He
loved her. After the deaths of her grandmother and
parents, she knew the only way she would ever be part
of a traditional family again was if she had one of her
own. At that time, she was on the downward side of
her mid-twenties, and she wasn't getting any younger.

She hadn't meant the Celebration's Bride contest to
be an ultimatum. Seriously she hadn't. She hadn't expected to win. So she told Josh she was entering and if
she won—*ha-ha*—he would have to marry her.

And holy moly, she'd won.

Josh ended up breaking up with her while the camera was rolling. They had captured every painful second of it on film. To rub salt into the wound, one of the
executive producers wanted to air the footage. Sydney,
her angel of mercy, had stopped that from happening.
Since then, the women had been fast friends.

As if Sydney hadn't done enough for her, Lily hoped

she could come through one more time and drive out and take her and the kids to get some gas. Then they could all get on with their day.

The last thing Lily wanted to do was interrupt Cullen at the hospital and ask him to come to her rescue. What kind of irresponsible person ran out of gas with a carful of kids?

"Hi, Syd, it's Lily. I'm so sorry to bother you, but I'm in a bit of a bind. It's ten-fifteen. Could you call me back as soon as possible?"

A sinking feeling told Lily that if Sydney hadn't picked up the phone, that probably meant she was busy. It would probably be a while.

Lily scrolled through her list of contacts, trying a few, but receiving voice mail after voice mail.

"Why don't you just call Uncle Cullen?" Megan insisted. "He'll come and get us. He told me that he would always be there for us if we ever needed him."

Lily didn't look up from her phone. "He is there for you, Megan. Your uncle Cullen is a very good man. I just don't want to bother him."

As a last resort, Lily dialed Kate Thayer's number. Kate was married to Liam Thayer, Cullen's colleague at the hospital. Liam and Kate had told her that Cullen was in need of a nanny.

"Hello, Lily?" Kate said. "How nice to hear from you."

After reaching so many voice mails, Lily felt her heart leaping at reaching a real live person.

"Oh, Kate, I'm so happy you picked up."

"What's going on?"

Lily explained the situation, sheepishly admitting she didn't have a subscription to a roadside-assistance program and that they hated to bother Cullen at the hospital.

"Not that I want to bother you," she said. "But is there any way you can help?"

"Lily, I'm so sorry, but I'm in New York on business. If I were there I'd be happy to help."

As the president of the Macintyre Family Foundation, Kate was in charge of a multimillion-dollar nonprofit organization. Of course she wouldn't be sitting around waiting for something to do or someone to rescue. But it had been worth a try.

"Thank you, Kate," Lily said. "I hope I didn't interrupt you."

"No, of course not," Kate said. "I'm happy you felt comfortable enough to call me. Hey, wait a minute. I have an idea. Let me call my office manager, Becca Flannigan. She might be able to meet you and take you to get some gas. Where are you?"

Before Lily could answer, the call-waiting tone sounded. Lily pulled the phone away from her ear and saw Cullen's name on the display screen. Her heart nearly leaped out of her chest; then her entire body went numb. For a fleeting moment she thought about not answering, but she knew that wasn't an option. "Kate, Cullen is beeping in. May I call you right back? Or better yet, so as not to bother you, why don't you just text me Becca's number and I'll call her? That way you won't have to be the middle person and you can get back to work."

"Sounds perfect," said Kate.

Lily thanked her again before ending the call and picking up Cullen's.

"Hello, Cullen?"

"Hi, Lily. Is everything okay? I just picked up an SOS text from Megan. She said you were stranded along the side of the road. I'm on my way to the car. Where are you?"

"Cullen, I'm so sorry about this," Lily said as he popped open the trunk of his car and removed the red gas can. "You didn't have to come all the way out here to rescue us. I had someone lined up to bring us some gas."

Rescue us. The words resonated with him and he felt the edges of his mouth turn up. He'd been so angry when he'd gotten the text from Megan, but standing here now, all his anger melted away. Lily Palmer was feminine and graceful, but something in her posture and the apologetic expression on her face told him she wasn't fond of being *rescued.* He wondered how much of her hesitancy over calling him stemmed from the kiss they'd shared last night.

"I told Megan we didn't want to bother you at work," Lily said. "I had someone lined up to bring us some gas. And where on earth did Megan get a cell phone? I had no idea she had one."

"It's a disposable phone," he said. "I got it for her to help her feel more secure. She and her siblings have been through so much change. I just thought it would help her feel better to know I was only a phone call away. A lifeline."

Lily's mouth formed a sympathetic O. "Of course," she said. "I didn't mean to be insensitive. I was just a little surprised."

"When I gave it to her, I told her it was for emergencies only. And since this would constitute an emergency, I'm glad she texted me. Why didn't you call me? You were stranded on the side of the road, Lily. Who knows what could've happened?"

His gaze snared hers for a second before she blinked and looked away.

"I didn't want to bother you."

"I'd rather you called than end up roadkill. Besides, I needed a break," Cullen said. "It's nice to get outside and away from the hospital for a change."

Lily looked at her cell phone. "At ten-thirty in the morning? It's nice of you to say that, but it's a little early for lunch."

"Not when your day starts at six-thirty," he countered. Then again, her day started even earlier since she was usually at the house a good half hour before he left. This morning things had felt a little awkward. Both of them had been distant. She'd been preoccupied and he had to admit he'd been in a hurry to get out the door.

Cullen wondered if she was thinking about that, too, as she crossed her arms in front of her.

"Even if you do break for lunch this early, I doubt this is how you wanted to spend your time. You hired me to make your life easier, not complicate it."

"Don't be ridiculous." His voice sounded gruffer than he'd intended. Again, he snared her gaze and held it for a few beats longer than what might be considered casual. This time she didn't look away. Not until he opened the car's fuel door and unscrewed the gas cap.

That was when he noticed four kid faces peering out from inside the SUV. Before Lily had gotten out of the car, she'd laid down the law and told the children that under no circumstances were they to get out of the car. Not on the highway. Thank goodness they seemed to be complying.

George pressed his face against the window so that his nose was flattened into a pig snout. As Cullen drained the gas into the vehicle, he tilted his head to the side and made a face back at George, extending his jaw so that his bottom teeth jutted out over his upper lip.

All four kids, even shy, subdued Bridget, seemed to find this hilarious and started making faces back at him.

Lily laughed. "What are they doing? And why are you egging them on?"

They shared the laugh.

When they were quiet again, Cullen said, "I must admit, I feel a little responsible for stranding you out here. You've got your hands full with the kids. I should've stopped and filled up the car before we got home last night."

Last night. Lily's cheeks flushed and she looked at a spot somewhere over his shoulder. "It's not your fault. I should've reminded you, but honestly, I didn't even think about it."

Her cheeks flushed a little more and he wondered if she was thinking about the kiss. Probably not.

Maybe.

It was cold outside and a little windy. Maybe that was what coaxed the color to her cheeks.

Cullen held up his hand. "Stop being so hard on yourself. You take great care of these kids. That's all that matters."

The kiss really hadn't been that big of a deal. Had it?

Sure, he had responded to the feel of her lips under his and to her sweet taste, hints of the vanilla and cinnamon she'd used in her baking. But maybe the taste had simply been his imagination, brought on by the power of suggestion.

Since she'd arrived, the entire house had been perfumed with good smells and warmed with Christmas cheer. It was all so different from what he was used to. She was so different from his usual *type*.

But he was glad that the kids had helped them along with the mistletoe prank.

"I didn't want to let the kids down," she said.

Her words jarred him from his thoughts back to the present. If he didn't know better, it was almost as if she'd been reading his mind.

"What?" he asked, screwing the gas cap back into place and shutting the small door.

"I didn't think you were listening." Lily smiled knowingly. "I was saying that we were on our way to Dallas to buy some shoes for George. The coach wouldn't let him on the court with dark-soled sneakers."

"Right," he said, as if he'd heard every word. He set down the canister and reached into his pocket for his wallet. "You'll need some money for that. You know, I don't ever expect you to pay for any of the kids' expenses. That shouldn't come out of your pocket."

As he handed her three crisp fifty-dollar bills, a sharp rapping sounded from the car window. George was at it again. This time, he'd smooshed his lips against the window and was moving them like a giant fish.

"Oh, George," Lily said. "Stop."

Of course, the kid couldn't hear her. He pulled his face back from the window and pressed his index fingers together, moving them in opposite directions in the international kid sign for two people kissing.

Lily gasped, then groaned.

"I'd better get the shoes so I can get him to camp so he can put some of this energy to good use. But first I'll fill up with gas so we don't run out again." Her face was bright red and she was stumbling over her words.

George must've seen the shocked embarrassment on Lily's face, because now he was alternately pointing at the two adults and making his fingers kiss.

"Oh, gosh," she said. "I'm so sorry, Cullen."

As she headed toward the driver's door, he said, "I'm not."

She turned back to face him, her hand on the car door, confusion eclipsing her earlier embarrassment. "What do you mean?"

"I'm not sorry I kissed you last night. Let George make all the faces he wants, or better yet, you can tell him to stop it. I understand that he's been through a lot, but that doesn't give him license to disrespect you. And for the record, I'm not sorry I kissed you, and if you're not sorry about that, I hope someday soon you'll let me kiss you again."

Chapter Six

It wasn't even a real kiss.

The kids had instigated it. So it didn't count, Lily reminded herself as she hitched her purse up onto her shoulder, adjusted her grip on the Secret Santa present she was bringing to girls' night out and walked toward Café St. Germaine in downtown Celebration to meet her girlfriends for dinner.

However, his confession that he'd like to kiss her again was as real as her thudding heart.

The temperature had dropped about ten degrees since this morning when Cullen had come to their rescue. Thinking about his parting words made her feel downright steamy. Her stomach somersaulted as she recalled the look in his eyes.

That look promised that the next kiss wouldn't be quite so innocent.

Her mind told her she was playing with fire, but her thudding heart said, *Bring it on;* she'd need something to keep herself warm during these increasingly cold nights Celebration was experiencing.

She'd never been able to see straight when it came to men. Never. That was why things had ended so badly with Josh. She'd ignored the signs, turned away from the hard reality that there were problems with their relationship and goaded him into the wedding.

When Josh had started to pull away, she'd thought that he was just overwhelmed by how fast and how public the wedding was moving forward. Cold feet. She'd convinced herself that once the hoopla was over they'd settle into married life and everything would be fine.

They'd been together for so long, marriage was just the next natural step along the way.

She'd been kidding herself, ignoring the handwriting on the wall, until everything had blown up in her face. Was that what she was doing now?

Convincing herself that this thing with Cullen might be heading somewhere when it wasn't? She really needed to think about that.

Common sense told her that getting involved with her boss was a bad idea. The kids needed her full attention. She needed the money. Otherwise she wouldn't even be here. If getting involved with Cullen was a good idea, wouldn't he be willing to hold that promised kiss until she was no longer on his payroll?

He might not.

If not, she had her answer.

Maybe he was only flirting with her.

The kids had put them in an awkward position with that mistletoe.

They'd handled it appropriately. But if it was all just a game, why had he said what he'd said today when he came to their rescue?

He didn't have to say that. She hadn't coaxed it out of him.

As she approached the restaurant's hostess stand, she shook away the thoughts and the nagging question of whether she should ask her girlfriends for advice.

Until she told someone what had happened, everything was safe. She could back out or move in whichever direction she wanted. But once she started asking for opinions and input, the situation would become very real.

"Hi, I'm Lily Palmer." She put her Secret Santa present on the hostess stand. "I'm meeting the James party of four tonight. I think I'm supposed to leave the gift here. Someone was going to deliver all the presents to the table once we're all seated to protect the identities of the respective Secret Santas."

The young woman smiled. "Of course. I'm happy to help you. That sounds like such a fun game."

It *was* fun, and it was so wonderful that this group of strong, smart women had welcomed her into their ranks. They'd been lifelong friends and jointly owned the Celebrations Inc. Catering Company. Sometimes infiltrating the ranks of an established friendship was impossible. Yet they'd welcomed her as if she'd always been one of their best friends.

"Ms. James and another person in your party are already seated," said the hostess. "Follow me and I'll take you to your table."

The restaurant was decorated beautifully with silver, gold and red decorations. Hundreds of gold fairy lights gave the place a festive feel. They were wrapped around wreaths of garland, swagged in doorways and wrapped around columns. Clusters of red ornaments were grouped with the miniature lights and displayed under glass domes as centerpieces. They'd transformed the already elegant restaurant into a festive place perfect for holiday gatherings such as this one.

Not only that, but the wood-burning oven made the place smell delectable. Lily's stomach growled in appreciation and she realized that she'd been so busy today that she hadn't eaten lunch.

Once she'd gotten George's shoes and had delivered him to camp, the girls had wanted grilled-cheese sandwiches for lunch. Knowing that she'd be dining out tonight—and there would likely be champagne and dessert involved—Lily had forgone the cheese and butter. They'd gotten so busy baking that before she knew it, it was time to pick up George. The kids had a snack. Then Cullen had gotten home.

Cullen.

Lily's stomach dipped at the thought of him.

He'd been prompt, getting home at exactly six as he'd promised when she'd told him about her night out. Maybe it was her imagination, but it seemed as if he'd been a little relieved when he learned that her dinner was with girlfriends.

That it wasn't a date.

She smiled to herself. Maybe she should've let him think it was a date.

There she went again. Living her own little fantasy rather than taking a good, hard, *real* look at what was really going on.

Sydney James and Pepper Macintyre waved from the corner table when they saw Lily enter the dining room.

"There they are," Lily said.

"Enjoy your evening," the hostess said, letting Lily walk the rest of the way to the table on her own.

Both women stood and hugged her.

"Merry Christmas," said Sydney.

"Hey, darlin'," Pepper said. "I was afraid we were going to have to drink this bottle of champagne all by our lonesome."

Lily glanced at her watch as her friends scooted in toward the center of the large booth to make room for her.

"I hope I'm not late," Lily said.

"Heavens no." Pepper poured Lily a flute of bubbly. "Whenever there's champagne, I'm always early. Besides, A.J. isn't even here yet."

"If she doesn't hurry," Sydney said, "all the champagne will be gone."

"Or we'll just order another bottle," Pepper said as she slid the cut-glass flute toward Lily and returned the bottle to the ice bucket.

Lily loved a lot of things about these women, but high on her list was the contrast between Sydney's proper British demeanor and Pepper's bubbly Southern-belle style.

Though Sydney had been born and raised in England, she'd come to Celebration by way of the European principality of St. Michel. Pepper, on the other hand, was a Texas belle through and through. From one of the most prominent families in Texas, she had withstood scandal of the worst kind when her father was convicted of fraud. He had eventually died in prison, leaving Pepper to reconcile the father she loved with the man who had become one of the most loathed people in the United States. Even though Pepper was innocent of her father's crimes, for a period of time she'd been a social pariah herself in the wake of the financial havoc her father's schemes had wreaked on innocent people.

Lily knew there was more to Pepper than her debutante appearance. She knew it had taken a strong woman to come out even stronger on the other side of the scandal that she'd had nothing to do with.

The three friends looked up and saw A.J. hurrying toward them, her arms full of Secret Santa presents. Usually calm and collected, A. J. Harrison looked a bit frazzled in her mad rush across the restaurant.

"I'm so sorry I'm late," she said, setting the wrapped packages on the table. "I had a hard time getting Kelcie down for the night. Shane is a great father, but she's getting to that stage where she's a mama's girl. I love the fact that she wants me, but on a night like this, I'd just like to be able to leave the house without both of us being in tears. I want to get out. I *need* to get out, but it breaks my heart when she cries like that."

Pepper drained the last of the bottle into a glass for A.J. and held it out to her. "Here, hon, drink this. It'll help. And I think another bottle is definitely in order."

A.J. settled herself in the booth and looked at her three friends. "Where is Kate? I thought she said she could make it tonight."

"Kate is out of town on business," Pepper informed her. Pepper was married to Rob, Kate's brother. So the two were as close as sisters. "A potential donor called late yesterday about making a year-end donation to the foundation and wanted to meet with her today. She was hoping to join us later, but she said not to count on her. So we should go ahead and order. If she can be here, she will. Don't worry. I brought her Secret Santa present."

"I hope she can join us." Sydney raised her glass. "But without further ado, I think a toast is in order. To good friends."

"Hear, hear!" they all said in unison. "To good friends."

They clinked glasses and had started debating the appetizer selections when Pepper said, "Before we order appetizers, why don't we open our presents? That will give us more room on the table."

They'd set a twenty-dollar limit for the gifts, and Lily had suspected it had been mostly for her benefit. Her friends could afford to spend much more, but they understood that finances were tight for Lily. They knew that was why she'd taken the nanny job rather than taking time off on her holiday break.

But what she lacked in funds, she'd tried to make up for in creativity with a beautifully wrapped package and a loaf of the stollen she, Megan, Bridget and Hannah had made.

They were having so much fun baking since she'd introduced them to her great-grandmother's recipe yesterday. The girls had been amazed that they could actually make their own bread.

"I thought you had to buy things like that in the store," Bridget had said. "I didn't know people could actually make bread at home."

The girls' wonder and excitement had Lily falling in love with them a little more. Once they'd gotten George settled at basketball camp, they'd decided to make as many loaves as they could to give as Christmas presents.

Lily had shown them variations on the traditional recipe they'd made yesterday and they'd been happy campers eager to try each one and had even suggested a few of their own concoctions after tasting Lily's recipes. The novelty was bound to wear off sooner or later, but for now it kept them busy.

When Lily and her friends had drawn names for the Secret Santa game, Lily got A.J., the one of her new friends that she knew the least about. So Lily was all for it when the girls had come up with the idea of giving the loaves of stollen as Christmas gifts. The girls had helped her make a special loaf to supplement the handblown glass ornament she'd purchased for A.J.

Sydney took charge, reading the gift tags and distributing the presents.

"I know this is silly," Pepper said, "but I get so excited when it comes to presents. I love to get them and I *love* to give them." She slanted a glance at Lily and flashed a knowing smile. Suddenly Lily had a pretty good idea of the identity of her own Santa.

All doubts were dispelled after she opened the small package and pulled out a beautiful sterling-silver bracelet with an infinity symbol strung between two delicate chains. The bracelet surely cost more than the twenty-dollar limit.

"This is gorgeous," Lily said. "Thank you so much."

When she struggled to put it on her wrist, Pepper helped her work the clasp.

As Lily held up her arm and admired the bracelet, she silently warred with herself. The bigger part of her was excited and grateful for the beautiful bracelet, but the smaller, more insecure part of herself was embarrassed that all she had to offer was a Christmas-tree ornament and a loaf of homemade bread.

Still, she'd always prided herself on being real. She'd never changed herself to fit in with anyone. Her friends knew of her circumstances and embraced her anyway. Now was not the time to change.

She appreciated the way that A.J. oohed and aahed over the ornament. It was pretty. But when her friend opened the festively printed cellophane bag that contained the stollen, Lily said, "You can save that for later."

"Are you kidding?" said A.J. "I'm starving and it looks delicious. Everyone can have a small piece."

A.J. sliced rough pieces with her butter knife, and when she bit into it, a look of rapture overtook her face. She closed her eyes as she chewed.

"Oh, my gosh," she said. "This is the best thing I have ever tasted." She looked directly at Lily, who had obviously given away her own Secret Santa identity when she'd suggested that A.J. save the bread for later. "What is this?"

The other girls offered their own appreciation.

"It's a Christmas bread that my grandmother and I used to make every year. It was always a tradition for us to make it together. Now it's just not Christmas without it."

Lily noticed that her friends were exchanging glances. They seemed to be communicating without saying anything. If Lily hadn't been so sure that the bread was indeed delicious, she might have been afraid of what they were communicating among themselves.

"Are you thinking what I'm thinking?" Pepper finally said aloud.

"I'm pretty sure I am," A.J. said as she twisted the open end of the cellophane and put the bread away. Lily wanted to think that A.J. liked it so much that she didn't want to share.

Sydney dabbed the corners of her mouth with her napkin before saying, "I think it's exactly what we've been looking for."

The three women nodded and turned to Lily. "How many loaves do you think you could produce in a day?"

"I don't know," Lily said. "Today, the girls and I baked six. But we were just having fun. They really enjoy baking."

Sydney's eyes flashed. "All the better. Lily, how would you feel about selling your bread at the holiday market? It's that big Christmas bazaar the city holds every year in the farmers'-market building. It opens next week. Celebrations Incorporated is sponsoring a booth and we're filming a segment of *Catering to Dallas* on opening day.

"The girls could help you bake, and if you're looking for something to keep them occupied, they could actually help out at the Celebrations Inc. booth."

At face value, it sounded like a wonderful, fun idea, but when you factored children into the mix, it changed the equation.

"It might be fun," she said. "I'll have to talk to Cullen and see how he feels about it."

The reality was that the girls were enamored with baking right now, but there was no telling when they would get tired of it and want to move on to something else. Lily would hate to promise something she couldn't deliver.

"How long will the holiday market be open?" she asked.

"It runs for a week, starting next week," said A.J. "I really do think your bread would be a hit. We'd sell out in a heartbeat."

"And there's nothing like scarcity to bolster an item's popularity," said Sydney, sounding very businesslike. "I would say, make what you can and if there is a greater demand, all the better."

"I'll bet the kids would be excited about it if they knew they were going to be on television," said Pepper. "I know our producers would love to feature them on the show."

Ordinarily Lily would've been excited for the kids. However, she remembered her own brush with near fame when she was supposed to be featured on the show as the winner of the Celebration's Bride contest. Her experience had been less than stellar. In fact, it had almost been the biggest nightmare of her life.

The only thing worse than being left at the altar was being dumped on national television.

While she knew her friends would only have the kids' best interest at heart, the memory of Lily's own experience still burned.

"Don't worry," said Sydney. "We'll pay you for the bread that is sold. If the kids want to work the booth, I'm sure we can pay them for their help, too."

Sydney was eyeing Lily as if she was trying to gauge her agreement. Pepper and A.J. nodded.

"Think about it and talk to Dr. Studly," Sydney said. "And let us know."

"Dr. Studly?" Lily asked, her girl parts loving the moniker.

"Yes! Don't you think that's an apt name for him?" Pepper asked as she reached for the lone package left in the center of the table. "He's gorgeous."

Just like that, Pepper steered the conversation in a different direction. Lily's heart sank. Her opening to talk about Dr. Studly had come and gone before she could seize the moment.

"I'll take this to Kate," Pepper said, putting the unopened package next to her purse. "Speaking of... Kate called the office this morning asking Becca to help you. Did you have car trouble this morning, Lily?"

Lily felt her cheeks heat. "Oh, that. I did. But it all worked out. It was very sweet of Kate to offer to help."

"Is that what your call to me was about?" Sydney asked. "But then you texted back that all was fine, that I didn't need to call you back. Was everything okay?"

Lily waved her off. "Everything was fine. I was a little concerned at first because I was out with the kids and it was so much colder this morning than it had been. But everything worked out. We're all safe and sound."

After Cullen had shown up, Lily had texted both Sydney and Becca, telling them not to worry, that the crisis was over and they didn't need to call her back.

She'd felt as if she'd been a big enough pain in the neck sending out the SOS in the first place; she wanted to minimize it as much as possible once she and the kids were safe and back on the road.

"So, what happened?" Sydney asked. "I'm so sorry I wasn't able to pick up when you called. I was in a meeting for the holiday market."

"No worries," she said. "Cullen rented an SUV for me to drive the kids. We had such a crazy morning that

I forgot to check the gas gauge and I ran out of gas. I feel so stupid. I mean, how irresponsible is that?"

For a split second she wondered if this would be a good segue into the kiss and the promise.

No. Maybe not.

Since Pepper and Kate were sisters-in-law and Kate was married to Liam Thayer, who worked with Cullen at the hospital, she didn't want to take the chance that Pepper, who was famous for being a good friend but not being able to keep a secret, might say something to Kate, who might say something to Liam, who in turn might tell Cullen.

She picked up the menu and pretended to study the appetizers.

This crush suddenly felt very schoolgirlish.

Still, she couldn't take the chance of embarrassing herself and making things any more awkward than they already were.

"So, who brought you the gas?" Sydney asked.

"Cullen did," Lily said. "I think the baked Brie and the margarita salad sound like good choices for appetizers. What do you think?"

She didn't even have to look up from the menu to know that three pairs of eyes were locked on her.

Oh, boy, she'd taken a wrong turn trying to play it off so nonchalantly.

"So, Dr. Studly, the renowned workaholic, took precious time out of his day to bring you some gas?" Pepper asked.

"He did."

There was expectation in the silence before A.J. finally said, "I'm happily married, but can we take a moment to acknowledge the indisputable fact that Cullen Dunlevy is hot? I'm just saying."

Yes! And he kissed me. And he wants to kiss me again.

All three women murmured and nodded appreciatively, as if A.J. had presented solid evidence for why Cullen should be named the eighth wonder of the world.

Lily would support that cause.

This was one of the reasons why she had become such fast friends with these women. They knew a good thing when they saw it.

"Stand in line, honey," said Pepper. "I hear there are a lot of women who appreciate Dr. Studly's attributes."

"As I said, I'm very happily married," A.J said. "Thank goodness I won't be lining up for an appointment with the good doctor."

"With that husband of yours?" Pepper said. "Dr. Studly doesn't hold a candle to him."

To each her own.

A.J. smiled a knowing smile that hinted that she knew exactly how lucky she was.

"I've heard he's got quite a reputation of being a love-'em-and-leave-'em ladies' man," Sydney offered.

"You're right about that." Pepper wrinkled her nose. "He's kind of a man whore. Kate was telling me some of the stories that Liam has told her about the illustrious Dr. Studly."

Pepper leaned in conspiratorially and the others followed. "I wouldn't trade Rob for anyone, especially not Cullen Dunlevy, but I must admit…" A mischievous smile curved up the corners of her mouth. "If you were single and not looking to settle down, wouldn't you be curious to know what makes all those women line up?

What would it be like to spend one night with the infamous doctor?"

Her friends, who were so lucky to have found the men of their dreams, laughed and offered some *I'm-not-saying-yes, I'm-not-saying-no* shoulder rolls and eyebrow quirks.

"How about you, Lily?" Pepper said. "You're not married. Let us live vicariously through you. Have you ever wondered what it would be like to spend a night in Dr. Studly's bed?"

Yes.

Lily was sure her face must be the same color as the ornaments in the centerpiece on their table. "There are too many kids around for me to think about anything other than being a nanny."

Liar.

The corner of Pepper's mouth quirked. "Oh, girl, you know what they say about all work and no play."

"Oh, I don't know," said A.J. "Really, would you want one night with the doctor if you knew someone else had been there the night before and would probably be taking your place right after you left?"

Lily bristled inwardly. "You all are making him sound like a hound dog."

"If the breed fits," A.J. offered. "I'm just saying, if the guy has a reputation, it had to come from somewhere. Who wants to be his number one if he has a number two? And it sounds like this guy might have them lined up into the double digits."

For some inane reason, Lily's impulse was to defend Cullen. "I know I haven't been there very long, but since I have, he's been a perfect gentleman. I've witnessed nothing to support your man-whore accusations."

But then she thought of that graphic text from Giselle.

Still, he hadn't gone out with Giselle that night.

He'd come home and they'd gone to get the Christmas tree. And he'd kissed her under the mistletoe.

She gave herself a sharp mental shake. Was she ever going to learn? Had she heard nothing that her friends had said? The man had a reputation for being a first-class womanizer. She had seen the handwriting on the wall with her own eyes. Or at least she'd seen the words in Giselle's text. It was a wonder she hadn't been blinded.

All the wishing and dreaming and imagining that Cullen was someone different than who he was wouldn't change him.

His admitting he wanted to kiss her again didn't mean he wasn't kissing others. And she certainly wasn't going to stand in line.

She wasn't Giselle. She'd never be Giselle.

So she might as well admit to herself that she and Cullen Dunlevy had nothing to offer each other and there was no sense in pretending otherwise.

Why had he told Lily he wanted to kiss her again? When had his libido decided to go rogue and take his filter with it?

It was the truth.

He'd love to taste her lips again. This time in a real kiss. A sensual joining of his mouth on hers, his hands on her body, exploring those curves that had driven him wild since the first day he'd opened the door and found her on his porch.

Now all he could think about was getting her in his bed.

He needed to get rid of that fixation. She was here for the kids, not for his pleasure. She wasn't like any other women who understood he couldn't give more than the short-term good time he was offering.

The women he dated understood him and he understood them and gave them exactly what they wanted. Lily hadn't asked for him to kiss her, although she'd kissed him back and hadn't complained.

She hadn't even rebuffed him when he'd mentioned that he'd like to kiss her again. Actually she hadn't said anything. She'd simply smiled and walked toward the van and gotten on with her day. He'd gotten on with his.

And that brought him full circle: she was way too good for him; she deserved much more than he could offer. She'd confirmed his suspicions that she was the marrying type. Hell, she'd been engaged once. Why had the guy let her go? She was a rare find for anyone who wanted that kind of life.

If he were smart, he'd stick to the Giselles and Evas and Candices of his world. The ones who knew and appreciated his no-strings-attached rules. He wouldn't fall into the trap of wanting what he shouldn't want, the way his father had.

His old man's lack of self-control had ruined a lot of lives, and Cullen wanted to be nothing like him. Still, he had his father's DNA, didn't he? He'd tried marriage and it hadn't worked. Thank God he and Brenda had been too busy with their careers to make kids a casualty of their mistake.

Lily wanted marriage and kids. She should have

them. It would be a crime for her not to be a mother and wife. She'd be damn good at it.

Cullen brooded in his leather club chair in his home office. He knocked back the rest of his glass of Scotch on the rocks, listening to the faint din of the television show that the kids were watching in the family room. Thoughts of his father knocked around his brain, bringing back bad memories Cullen would prefer to let go.

Having the kids and Lily here had excavated them.

But this was the reality check he needed.

Lily had been engaged once. It hadn't worked out. He had no idea what she expected from future relationships. Their talk had been brief and he hadn't had the time to learn what she liked, what turned her off, what she expected from the men she dated. Hell, for all he knew, he might not even be her type.

But he had pretty good instincts, and his instincts told him that she was traditional and looking for a committed, white-picket-fence-kids-and-dog kind of life.

He wasn't the man who could offer her that.

The phone rang, pulling him out of his brooding.

His first thought was *Lily?*

He'd thought of her first. Before the hospital. She was off the clock. Why would she be calling him when she hadn't been able to bring herself to call him today when she and the kids had needed help?

He got up and went to his desk to check the caller ID. It was a number he didn't recognize, so he let it go to voice mail.

As soon as the message flashed on the screen, he picked it up.

"Hey, stranger," came the familiar voice. "I'll bet

I'm the last person you thought would be calling tonight. But it's me."

Brenda? He became instantly wide-awake.

I'll be damned.

It was as if his thoughts about marriage had conjured her, the only woman in the world he'd ever allowed to tempt him into violating his no-commitments rule. Except for the wayward thoughts he'd been having about Lily. The nanny. God, a shrink would have a field day with that one. Textbook 101. Sexual fantasy: doing the nanny.

He felt a pang of regret, ashamed of himself for even thinking of Lily in that context. She deserved better.

And how ironic that his ex-wife, Brenda, had called to subliminally remind him of that.

His marriage to Brenda had lasted a few months shy of two years before they'd called it quits.

"Well, babe," the message continued. "I'm going to be in town soon and I wanted to see you. Actually there's a chance you may be seeing a whole lot more of me whether you want to or not. There's a practice in Celebration looking to take on a partner. So give me a call. I want to get together for dinner."

She left her number, then sighed. It was an uncharacteristic sound for her, a lot more wistful and sentimental than Brenda had ever sounded when they were together.

"Call me, okay?"

She paused.

"I've been thinking about you, Cul. I miss you."

Chapter Seven

"Do you have a moment?" Lily asked Cullen.

She was standing there in the kitchen, with her purse on her shoulder and her coat on her arm.

For you, I have all night.

It was true, but Cullen was sure that Lily wouldn't appreciate the context in which he was thinking. "Of course. Is everything all right?"

She set her purse on the counter. Cullen pulled out a chair for her and motioned for her to sit down.

"Thank you," she said.

He sat down in the seat next to her, angling his chair so that he faced her. "What's on your mind?"

He forced his gaze not to stray to her lips. That full bottom lip. She was saying something, but he couldn't really concentrate.

"So, what do you think?" Lily asked. She paused a moment. He blinked at her. *Busted.*

"You didn't hear a word I just said, did you?"

No, he hadn't. Because he'd been too busy thinking about things he'd thought he had already dismissed. Last night, after he called Brenda back and agreed to have dinner with her when she got to town, he'd talked himself into enforcing strict boundaries for himself where Lily was concerned.

When he started feeling odd about making plans with Brenda, he realized those lines needed to be not only drawn but strictly observed.

When was the last time he'd felt odd about doing anything? What was it about this woman that fogged his usually clear head and disconnected the circuits in his brain?

Still, he flashed his most disarming smile at her, the one that usually got him out of hot water with other women. Somehow he knew this wouldn't work with her. She was warm and smart and funny…and she had a heart the size of Texas when it came to those she cared for, and right now she was rolling her eyes at his obvious lack of focus.

"Last night when I had dinner with my girlfriends," she said, probably repeating herself. He listened this time. "They invited the kids and me to help them out at the holiday market. They're even willing to pay the kids so they can earn a little spending money of their own. You know, this is the weeklong holiday bazaar that they have at the farmers' market every year in December. Have you ever been? It's so much fun."

He shook his head. "I know what you're talking about, but I've never been. I guess I've always been working when it's been going on. Do the kids want to do it?"

"I haven't said anything to them because I wanted to ask you first," she said.

He thought he glimpsed something that looked like hesitation in her eyes.

"I appreciate that," he said. "Since I've never been, do you think they'd enjoy it?"

"Well, the girls have been crazy about all the baking we've been doing," she said.

"I know," Cullen said. "Thanks to all that great baking, I've had to loosen my belt buckle a few notches. If it means that you'll be selling the bread rather than having it around the house, by all means, sign them up. It's just too hard to resist."

Just like you.

He checked the wayward thoughts, especially when he saw the look on Lily's face. "Don't get me wrong, I love everything that you and the girls have made. I just like it a little too much for my own good."

He patted his stomach to keep his gaze from falling to those lips that were driving him to distraction.

"You do know that the company that my friends own, Celebrations Incorporated, is featured on that television show *Catering to Dallas,* right?"

"Yes." Again, he'd heard of it, but he'd been too busy to watch it.

"They're going to be filming an episode of the show during the holiday market."

Her brow was knit and he could tell something wasn't setting right with her. "Is that a problem? Is there a reason we should be concerned about it?"

"I wish I could say no." She hesitated.

"They're your friends, aren't they? They wouldn't

put the kids in a situation that wouldn't be in their best interest, right?"

"They wouldn't," she said. "I can guarantee you that, but it is a reality television show and programs like that thrive on drama, even if it's manufactured."

"How much drama could a reality show about a catering company generate? Especially if it's set at a family-friendly holiday market. Sounds about as wholesome as it gets."

Lily was still frowning.

"Is there something you're not telling me?"

"Last year, I was supposed to be featured on the show," Lily said.

"Supposed to be?" Cullen asked. "What happened?"

Lily bit that beautiful bottom lip and looked a little pensive. "Remember how I told you I was supposed to get married?"

He nodded.

"I won a contest called Celebration's Bride. My fiancé, Josh, and I won an all-expense-paid wedding and reception that was supposed to be aired on the show."

"What happened?"

"Josh decided he didn't want to get married after all."

"I'm sorry."

She waved away his condolence.

Actually he was sorry for the guy who'd lost out— he was an idiot to let a woman like Lily get away. But then again, Cullen knew all too well that not everyone was built for the traditional married lifestyle. It was too bad that Lily had to be the one to suffer from it. Obviously talking about it upset her.

"Josh and I wanted different things," she said. "I

want marriage and a family of my own. He didn't. But you don't need to hear my sob story. That's not why I brought it up. The producers of *Catering to Dallas* managed to be lurking when Josh backed out of the wedding. They got it on film and wanted to air the footage. The only reason they didn't was my friend Sydney. She managed to get them to pull the segment. I just want to make sure that the kids aren't exposed to any surprises like that. They've been through enough in the past few months.

"I truly believe my friends would have the kids' best interest at heart, but they had no control over what happened to me. I don't want to take a chance of an overly ambitious producer pulling something that might make the kids uncomfortable."

He really couldn't have found a better person to care for the children. Lily *truly* cared.

His heart twisted as he thought of the humiliation she'd suffered, even if the breakup hadn't been broadcast on national television. This guy shouldn't have put her through it.

"I'm sorry that happened to you," he said. "No one should be treated like that."

She nodded. "It's very kind of you to say that."

His mind flashed back to what he'd said to her when he brought the gas to her the other day. How he hadn't regretted kissing her and that he wanted to do it again. If he wanted to be as kind as Lily was giving him credit for, he would never mention kissing her again. In fact, he wouldn't even think about it. She'd said it herself: she wanted a husband and a family. He had no intention of getting married again. Why lead her on a path that was contrary to everything she wanted?

"I know you only want what's best for the kids. So I'll trust your judgment on what to do about the holiday market and including them in the filming of *Catering to Dallas*."

He wished he could trust his own judgment when it came to her.

Adorned for the annual holiday market, the building that usually housed the farmers' market looked like a winter wonderland.

Vendors, as far as the eye could see, were selling everything from gifts to decorations to food and wine. From handmade candy canes and marshmallows to hot chocolate and mulled cider to holiday hors d'oeuvres and catered gourmet meals, to decorating services to all-out party planning.

Colorful lights were strung from corner to corner; glittering snowflakes hung from fishing line attached to the ceiling. In one corner of the large room stood the tallest tree that Lily had ever seen in her life. Underneath it, packages of all shapes and sizes were wrapped in colorful paper and decorated so attractively someone would have to be a complete Scrooge not to be tempted to pick up each one and shake it. In another corner was a big thronelike chair, painted gold and surrounded by a white picket fence swagged with fresh pine garland festooned with pinecones, silver bells and glittering red ornaments. At the entrance to the area, there was a sign that read North Pole This Way. Right next to the sign, a red carpet led to the chair.

Santa's chair.

Born and raised in Celebration, Texas, Lily had seen the big man sit there many Christmases. As soon as the holiday market opened for business, there would be a line out the door for kids to have a chance to see Santa Claus and tell him what they wanted for Christmas this year.

Even though she was thirty years old and it had been a long time since she'd sat on Santa's lap, Lily still got excited at the festive spectacle that was the holiday market.

This year was even more special since she was sharing it with Cullen and the children. They sort of felt like…a family.

The thought warmed Lily from the inside out.

As Lily, Cullen and the kids—even George—walked into the room the night before the market officially opened—for a special VIP vendor and sponsor party—it was even more exciting to get a behind-the-scenes glimpse of the place. To Lily, attending this party tonight was like being allowed on the set of the remake of a favorite movie.

"What was the number of the booth again?" Cullen asked, glancing around.

He had been wonderful when Lily broached the subject of the kids participating in the market. But in her heart she'd known that he would be good about it. He would do anything for those kids and he trusted her to do right by them.

Even though she'd been burned before by circumstances, she had decided to trust her friends. What was the chance of lightning striking twice?

It was a good lesson that she could apply to herself, too. She had been burned once in love. She wasn't going to let that keep her from finding the true love that she was sure was out there for her.

She stole a glance at Cullen. He flashed her a sexy grin, and her pulse quickened. He'd gotten off work early—well, early for him; it was nearly seven o'clock now—to come to the party with her and the kids. The commonsense, rational side of her figured he might be here so he could have a look at the setup and assess whether he felt comfortable letting the kids spend the week here.

But the hopeless romantic in her just couldn't give up hope that he was here for another reason: because he wanted to be. Because he wanted to spend time with the kids…and her. That maybe, just maybe, this would be the night that he made good on that promise to kiss her again.

But not in front of the kids, of course. She knew that he understood that, and she admired him for it. He had the makings of such a good father, and he could be one to these kids if he'd just give himself a little credit.

He'd helped them take their minds off their own tragedy and look outside themselves. The girls had told him about Stollenfest and how in Dresden they sold the Christmas bread to raise money for those less fortunate. The kids had decided they wanted to do that with the money they raised at the holiday market. He'd promised them he would match every dollar they raised. He even helped them pick out a charity: Grace Children's Home.

Lily's heart nearly burst when, as they were baking that morning, Megan shared the agreement that Cullen had struck with them.

She'd sounded so grown-up. "Because, you know, Lily, there are kids out there who are less fortunate than we are. We have you and Uncle Cullen, but some kids have nobody. We want to help them."

Lily was so touched she had to blink back tears.

After all the loss and turmoil they'd been through, they could still count their blessings. She realized that Cullen might have had a little something to do with that.

Actually he'd had everything to do with it. She could see that as plain as day. The one thing she was having trouble seeing was the bad boy that her girlfriends had described.

Sure, he was a complex, complicated man, and he'd obviously known more than his share of women, but he hadn't brought any of them around since she'd been caring for the kids. In fact, if she hadn't seen the text from Giselle, she might be inclined to believe that he'd gotten a bum rap with this bad reputation. Because all she knew was that he had such a big heart when it came to these children.

Whether he believed it or not, he would make a great father to these kids. Somehow she just had to make *him* recognize that side of himself.

As they approached the Celebrations Inc. booth, George stumbled and dropped the armload of loaves he was carrying. With a scowl, he bent down to pick them up, but an older lady who had been walking toward them stopped to help.

"There, there, let me help you, young man," she said, stacking the two remaining loaves on top of the ones he had already picked up.

"Thank you," Lily and Cullen said at different intervals. Their arms were already full and it would've been difficult to help George before they'd set down their loads.

"My pleasure," she said. "What are you selling?"

"Stollen Christmas bread," said Hannah.

"It's not *stolen*," Megan quickly informed the woman. "Like, we didn't steal it or anything. It's just called *stollen* because—because it's from Germany and that's what they call it. But we made it ourselves. We didn't take it from anyone."

"We're going to give the money we make selling it to kids who are less fortunate than we are," said Bridget, her voice barely a whisper.

The woman's hand fluttered to her heart. "That's the sweetest thing I've ever heard. I will certainly make sure I come back and buy several loaves to help you in your generous endeavor."

As the kids ran over to the Celebrations Inc. booth, the woman beamed at Lily and Cullen. "Such a beautiful family. The two of you are to be commended for raising such nice, civic-minded children."

Lily and Cullen exchanged a bemused look, but the woman didn't seem to notice. Neither one corrected her. To Lily, for one perfect, snow-globe moment, they *were* a family and it was everything she had ever wanted in the world.

"Oh, will you look at me, running my mouth while the two of you are standing there indulging me so politely? You have your arms full," the woman said. "Please don't let me keep you. I'll be back to buy some of that *stollen* bread before it gets away. Ta!"

She gave a fluttery wave of her fingers as she turned and walked away. Once they had unloaded the bread at the booth and the woman was out of earshot, Cullen turned to Lily and said, "There you go. Your first customer."

"Apparently so," Lily said, thinking he was going

to politely ignore the woman's mistaking them for a married couple.

Probably for the best.

"Would my *wife* care to help me carry in the rest of the bread from the car?"

Her pulse quickened and her breath caught in her chest. But she had enough of her wits about her to realize she'd better be cool. He was just playing along. They were flirting in that way that the two of them did so well.

She cocked an eyebrow at him, determined to let him interpret her response however he chose. But Cullen's suggestive stare held hers until she wanted to squirm. So she did the only thing she could do—she rolled her eyes at him.

He laughed.

"Hey, Syd, do you mind if we leave the kids with you while we go get the rest of the stollen?" Lily asked in a forced casual tone. "If we both go, one more trip to the car should do it."

"Good heavens," Sydney said. "You must've been baking nonstop since we agreed to do this."

"You have no idea." Cullen put his arm around Lily. "My wife is quite a talented baker."

Sydney's mouth opened as if she wanted to say something, but she closed it before she did. A look of bemused intrigue transformed her pretty face. She darted a glance at Lily that seemed to demand, *You will explain this later.*

"Your *wife,* huh?" she finally said.

"Oh, he's just kidding." Lily wiggled out from under Cullen's arm, hating the blush she was certain colored her cheeks.

Sydney seemed to be looking at them differently now. "Sure, you two lovebirds go get the rest of the stollen. I'll keep an eye on your kids for you, but don't do anything I wouldn't do. Cullen, I'm serious. She's my friend."

Cullen nodded and gave Sydney a little salute as he and Lily turned and walked toward the exit. Lily couldn't tell if he was being irreverent or if it was just his way of saying, *I understand.*

"What was that about?" he asked.

"Oh, you know Sydney," Lily said. "I think she fancies herself the big-sister sort who is looking out for me."

"I didn't realize you needed someone to watch over you."

Something flickered in his eyes, and her heart gave a tug. *Oh, you have no idea.*

"It never hurts to have someone in your corner," she said. And she wasn't sure if she was speaking about herself or the kids.

Maybe both. Probably both.

She decided that the safest thing to do was change the subject.

"So, speaking of wives…" Lily said. "I do believe we started a conversation at the tree lot the other night that we agreed would be continued."

"Did we?" he said.

Lily shoved his arm good-naturedly. "You know we did. We had a deal. I showed you mine. Now it's your turn to show me yours."

Her hand flew to her mouth. *I did not just say that.*

But, oh, yes…yes, she did. Because it was so foreign and contrary to how she normally acted and because of the priceless look on Cullen's face, it felt absolutely exhilarating.

As they walked, his arm brushed hers and the contact intensified the electric current already pulsing between them. "Well, heaven forbid I should ever renege on a deal. Especially one like that. What would you like to know?"

"Don't make me ask questions. Just give me the scoop. You know, like what happened? Why did you divorce?"

He drew in a deep breath and the energy between them seemed to shift and decrease several decibels. Maybe this wasn't such a good idea after all. In fact, in hindsight, it had the potential to kill the mood. Funny thing that—there was a fine line between intimacy and TMI.

Now she wished she could take it back and just continue to flirt. She really was an amateur at this, wasn't she?

"What happened?" he repeated, as if weighing his words. "We were both too focused on our jobs. It just didn't work out."

"What does she do?"

"She's a pediatric surgeon. And a darn good one, too."

Of course she was.

She was smart, and given Cullen's track record, she was probably beautiful, too.

"When we finished our residency, she got a pediatric-surgery fellowship in Seattle," he said. "I'd been offered the job here."

Lily resisted the urge to ask him if he'd fought for her. *Every woman needs to know the man she loves is willing to fight for her. That he won't just watch her walk away.*

Of course, Josh hadn't simply watched; he'd given her a great big shove.

"We met during our residency and got married," Cullen said. "We were married less than two years when she was awarded the fellowship. My work was here and hers was in Seattle. There wasn't much left to debate."

"You couldn't make it work long distance? A lot of couples do."

"She didn't want to."

Yes, but did you? And if so, did you fight for her?

Lily was dying to ask these questions, but she couldn't get the words out of her throat. He looked so vulnerable, so vastly different from the ladies' man her friends had made him out to be.

"It's interesting that we're talking about her. I hadn't heard from her in ages. That's what happens to two divorced workaholics who have no kids. Clean break. Move on."

That had been the case with her and Josh. They hadn't spoken since the breakup. And they lived in the same city.

"She called me a couple of nights ago."

Lily's stomach dropped. *What?* "Really? Just like that? Out of the blue?"

As they exited the building into the parking lot, she tried to get a read on how he felt about this, but she couldn't tell. He just looked uncomfortable.

"Seemingly, but she had a reason. She might be moving back. She's going to be in Dallas soon, talking to a pediatric practice about joining them."

"How nice." Lily's voice sounded pinched, but she

did her best to keep a smile firmly in place. "When will she be here?"

"She doesn't know yet. She's going to call me once she has firm dates."

He shrugged. She nodded.

"Actually it could be a good thing," Lily said, mustering all her courage. This...*this* was why she needed to remember her place. She was the nanny. He was her boss. "If you two got back together, you could keep the kids. You could be their parents."

Cullen snorted. "That will never happen."

Lily stopped just short of the SUV. If looks could kill, she would've skewered him with a death glare.

"They're good kids, Cullen," she snapped. "Especially given all that they've been through."

"Of course they are. I know that."

"You have plenty of room in your house. I don't understand why you wouldn't take them in."

"I don't have room in my life for four kids. It wouldn't be fair to them."

"But you're doing such a good job with them. Would it really be so different than it is now? I mean *right now*. Look at how happy they are and *she'd* be able to help you out."

The words had poured out of her as if someone had turned on the tap. Lily's heart pounded in her chest. As she grabbed the last of the stollen loaves, taking care not to reach in when Cullen did to avoid physical contact, she knew she should stop pushing the issue.

"We never wanted kids," he said. "That was one of the few things we did agree on."

He really didn't want kids? Even after spending nearly two weeks with the Thomas kids? The truth slapped her in the face. She deserved it. He'd told her this about himself how many times now?

Yet she still believed the kids would change him.

"She's a pediatrician and she doesn't want kids? Isn't that against the law of everything that's natural? Or at least against the oath she had to take as a kids' doctor?"

He shrugged again, and she knew they'd better steer the conversation to neutral territory. Especially since he hadn't denied the unspoken possibility of getting back together with her.

Her.

Lily hadn't even asked her name. He hadn't offered it. That was fine. She didn't want to know. Lily felt sick to her stomach. But better to know now than to get in any deeper than she already was. Really, she should thank him for this.

She forced another smile as he closed the SUV's hatchback. "I was so proud of the kids when they told me they want to donate the money they made selling the stollen to charity. And I was even more touched when I found out that you're going to match their donation. That's really great of you, Cullen."

As they walked back to the building, she purposely didn't look at him. Her heart needed more time to set after turning to jelly thanks to the news about his ex-wife. If she let him back in too soon, she risked it seeping out of her chest and spilling on the floor.

"It's the least I can do. But really, in the grand scheme of things, it's nothing. It's the time of year when we *should* be charitable. Or at least *I* should. I know I should be benevolent all year long, but—" He shrugged. "I get the idea that being altruistic is just your nature."

She slanted him a glance but took care not to let

her gaze linger. "Well, I'm a teacher by trade. I guess being charitable comes with the territory. But you... you're really good with them, Cullen. They *love* you so much."

There it was again. Words flowing like water. Like a babbling brook, as Josh used to say.

Josh had such a mean streak.

Still, she clamped her lips together to keep from saying anything else. She'd already used the word *love*.

Out of her peripheral vision, she saw Cullen roll his shoulder again. "I'm just doing right by Greg. He and Rosa were the ones who raised the kids right. I'm just continuing what they started. It's weird, thinking that they're gone. It makes you realize just how damn short life is. It makes you step back and take inventory of what's important and what isn't."

Somehow he managed to shift the loaves he was carrying—twice as many as she held—and open the door. She made the mistake of looking him in the eye. For a second that seemed to last an eternity, his hazel eyes were filled with pain and torment and something else that she couldn't quite define.

She looked down and stepped inside.

Oh, but he was a complicated one.

"They're just with me until I can find a family that will take all four of them. They have to stay together. I won't let them be broken up."

"And you really believe you can accomplish this before the first of the year?"

He nodded resolutely. "I have Cameron Brady working on it. He's a family-law attorney. I have every confidence in him that he will rise to the challenge and find a good place for them."

She followed Cullen's gaze to where the kids were inside the booth, helping Sydney and A.J. arrange the loaves they'd already brought in.

"They *are* great kids," he said. "They deserve so much more than I can give them. Besides, you make it so that all I have to do is show up. You're not always going to be here."

His voice faltered and he cleared his throat. "I mean you won't always be around, making everything so… right."

Her impulse was to say, *I can stay. All you have to do is ask me.* But she knew the real meaning behind the urge. She bit the insides of her cheeks to keep from blurting it out. She had a career of her own. And if *she*—the ex-wife—moved back in…

He was right about these kids needing stability. They needed a traditional home like what they were used to, where they felt comfortable and welcomed and loved. Even though no one could ever replace their mother and father, they needed the safety and sanctuary of a home with a man and a woman who loved each other. The girls needed a mom, and George, poor George… He was in such desperate need of a father figure.

"They told me you taught them about making donations," Cullen said. "You're the one who is setting the good example. They said you told them about a big festival in Germany where they sell baked goods to raise money for charity. The donation was their idea, but you planted the seed."

"Well, I think you underestimate how good you are with them—"

"Yoo-hoo! Yoo-hoo!" The voice came from behind them. When they turned around they saw the woman who had helped George pick up the bread rushing toward them.

"I'm so happy I caught you before you left," she said.

"We weren't leaving," Cullen said. "We were just going to get the final load of bread."

She smiled as she shook her head. "Parents' work is never done, is it? This world needs more families like you. Responsible, community-minded, raising your kids to be good citizens, too. Oh! How could I be so rude? I didn't even introduce myself. My name is Joan Cotton. I'm the chairwoman of the Jingle Bell Ball. Have you heard of it?"

"Cullen Dunlevy," he said. "And this is Lily."

It didn't escape Lily that Cullen hadn't said her last name. Was he purposely preserving the illusion that they were married? But they'd just talked about his ex-wife.

That put things into perspective.

"Of course I've heard of it," said Cullen. "The ball raises money for the New Harvest Food Bank. I've been to your event in the past."

Joan clapped her hands. "Yes! Are you going this year?"

"I must confess, it's been so hectic lately that I haven't purchased tickets."

Joan nodded. "As chairwoman of the ball, I like to give tickets to a handful of deserving couples. I would love for you to be my guest this year."

She held out an envelope to Cullen, but he hesitated.

"I'm happy to purchase the tickets." He frowned.

Lily took a step back. She'd just started to suggest that they continue on to the booth and not only lay down their load of stollen, but also relieve Sydney from child-care duties, when Joan jumped in.

"Giving away the tickets serves double duty. Not only does it raise awareness of New Harvest, but it gives a lovely, deserving couple like you a night out away from the kids. It's just something I like to do during the holidays. Of course, if you'd rather purchase them, I'm happy to carry your check back to the offices."

Lily saw what the woman was doing. She thought they were married. She was getting the wife's hopes up about attending the ball and putting the husband in a position where he couldn't refuse. This was guerrilla salesmanship at its finest. Ticket sales must have been low this year.

Lily braced herself for Cullen to politely refuse Joan. The best way for him to get out of this was to simply tell the woman that they not only weren't married, but weren't a couple, and they'd have no use for the tickets.

"Don't worry. There will be a silent auction and plenty of other opportunities for you to donate if you wish. So, please be my guest. Take your beautiful wife to the ball. You two deserve a romantic night out."

"May I bring you a check tomorrow?" Cullen asked.

Joan nodded eagerly.

Then he turned to Lily. "What do you say, *honey?* Would you be my date to the ball?"

Chapter Eight

During the week it was open, the holiday market closed at five o'clock Monday through Wednesday. The earlier hours allowed the vendors time to restock and rest up for the days of heavier shopping traffic and later hours on Thursday through Sunday.

Tonight, Wednesday, Lily had planned on getting together with Sydney, who was going to let her try on some gowns in her wardrobe that would be suitable for Lily to wear to the ball.

As a single schoolteacher on a limited budget, Lily didn't have any formal wear in her closet. Aside from prom dresses, her wedding gown was the fanciest dress she'd ever owned—or almost owned. When the wedding fell apart, she'd given back the dress, which had been part of the prize package she'd forfeited when she and Josh called their engagement off.

She'd never attended a ball before. Despite her excitement, right now she simply couldn't afford to spend a lot of money on a dress she'd probably wear once in her lifetime.

Once again, Sydney was coming to her rescue, playing fairy godmother to her Cinderella, Lily thought as she rang the doorbell of the sprawling Texas-ranch-style house that Sydney shared with her movie and television director husband, Miles Mercer.

"Hello, love," Sydney said after opening the wooden front door.

"I hope you're hungry." Lily held out the nine-by-thirteen-inch pan of lasagna she'd put together after she and the kids got home from the market. "There's plenty, so I hope Miles will join us. You'll still have leftovers that might come in handy since we'll be working late this weekend."

Actually Lily had made a double batch of lasagna, a pan to take with her and one so that Cullen and the kids would have a nice meal when they sat down to dinner together tonight. Cooking dinner for him and the kids had never been part of the plan, but they all had to eat anyway. And Cullen always invited her to stay and eat with them. At first she'd been hesitant. Now it was becoming their routine.

She wondered what the girls would say if they knew Cullen Dunlevy had curtailed his philandering in favor of family-style dinners.

He always seemed so appreciative, and she had to admit, she loved seeing the look on his face as he enjoyed her home-cooked meals.

"Actually Miles is out of town on a shoot tonight," she said. "So it's just us."

All the better. Right now Sydney was the only person who knew that Cullen was taking Lily to the ball. She'd let the others know eventually, but since the dance was nearly two weeks away, Lily didn't see the need to raise their eyebrows. Not right away, at least. Her friends were great, but she didn't want to hear their warnings or cautionary tales about Cullen.

"That smells delicious," Sydney said, ushering Lily into the kitchen. "I was going to suggest we order in, but this is even better."

Even though Sydney worked for Celebrations Inc. Catering, everyone knew she wasn't a cook. She handled public relations for the company, of which she owned a quarter. She was just as good in the public-relations office as A.J. was in the kitchen. It was a business partnership made in heaven.

"All I have to do is warm it up for about a half hour," Lily said.

"Help yourself to the oven," Sydney said. "That is so not my territory. I'm lucky to have friends and a husband who cooks."

Sydney paused and gave her a knowing stare. "I'd say a certain Dr. Studly is pretty lucky to have you. How's that going?"

"How is what going?" Lily feigned ignorance as she punched the buttons on the oven to start it preheating.

"You know exactly what I'm talking about," Sydney said, hands on her hips. "The big date. The reason you're here tonight—to look gorgeous for Prince Charming when he escorts you to the ball."

"First of all, it's not a *big date,*" Lily said. "We're just going. As friends. Joan Cotton gave us tickets and we didn't have the heart to refuse her. She was so nice about it."

"Yeah, she thought you were married," Sydney said. "I don't recall either of you setting her straight. In fact, what I do remember is Prince Studly looking pretty smug about it. I think he has his eye on you. And, Lily…"

Sydney frowned and Lily knew what was coming before she could even finish her statement.

"Just be careful, okay?"

"I'll be just fine. In fact, I'll be even better if I can try on the dresses before we eat. I don't relish the thought of trying to slip into a slinky gown after indulging in a big plate of pasta. I might get stuck. Actually you're a lot smaller than I am. Are you sure you have something that will fit me?"

"Don't be ridiculous," Sydney said. "Of course I do. You have a great figure. Come on. Let's go back to the bedroom and I'll show you what I've laid out for you."

Lily's mind tried to take her back to the past. It tried to dredge up every insecurity she'd ever felt about her curvy figure and compound it with the very real fear that nothing Sydney had to offer would fit. She'd be embarrassed and back at square one. But she wasn't allowing herself to go there.

Nope, worry was like paying on a debt you might never owe. She'd heard that somewhere and it had become her mantra. So she did her best to brush off the nagging doubts and followed her friend through an elegantly decorated living room, down a hardwood hallway and finally into one of the largest master suites she'd ever seen.

She'd been to Sydney and Miles's house numerous

times, but this was the first time she'd seen the master bedroom. Sydney had laid out at least a dozen gowns of various colors, cuts and levels of sparkle and bling.

As Lily took it all in, Sydney held up the arts and entertainment section of the *Celebration Daily News*. "Did you see the great article they did on the holiday market? There's a picture of the kids on page eight."

Sydney handed it to her. Lily perused the story on the first page before turning to page eight.

When she and the kids had gotten home from the market today, Lily had barely enough time to get the kids situated and the lasagnas made before Cullen got home. They'd talked for a bit—nothing dramatic or earth-shattering, just easy conversation about each of their days: his at the hospital and hers with the kids at the market—before she'd rushed to get over to Sydney's house. She hadn't had time to read the paper.

But there it was, a great picture of the girls smiling as Megan handed a loaf of stollen to a customer. The caption under the picture talked about how the children would donate the money they made from sales of the homemade bread to the Grace Children's Home.

"That's such a sweet picture," Sydney said.

"Isn't it? The girls will be so thrilled to see it." She had just started to close the paper when a familiar face caught her eye and made her do a double take.

She gasped. Because there smiling up at her from the section featuring the engagement announcements was her ex-fiancé, Josh Stockett, with a pretty, petite blonde. They'd been photographed in a posture Lily and her friends used to jokingly call the "awkward prom pose," where the couple had their arms around each other and their free hands were intertwined. The petite blonde's name, Lily learned after reading on a bit, was Ann-Elizabeth Hardy, daughter of Dr. Bernard and Daphne Hardy. Ann-Elizabeth—her name was hyphenated, so Lily was just sure she went by both names. Not Ann. Not Elizabeth. Certainly not Liz or Lizzy or, heaven forbid, Beth or Betsy. She was beautiful and thin with sorority-girl posture and a perfect toothy smile.

She was exactly the type Josh liked. And she was gazing up at the idiot as if he were the second coming.

Engaged.

Josh Stockett, the man whom Lily had had to goad into engagement, was finally getting married.

When Josh broke up with her, he'd originally told her he wasn't marrying her because she was too heavy. At a size twelve, he'd told her, he didn't want to risk getting stuck with a *fatty* and he'd bailed as fast as he could.

The memory made Lily's heart ache. Not for the loss of the man she'd once thought she wanted to spend the rest of her life with, but because she'd truly believed he'd loved her. Just the way she was.

She'd been traumatized.

It had taken her months to put everything into perspective. She'd never be a small woman. She loved to cook. Of course she wanted to be healthy, but she wasn't going to weigh every ounce of food she put in her mouth and she wasn't going to deny herself the foods she loved to cook and eat.

The truth of the matter was, Lily was comfortable in her own skin. Some women might've gone on a starvation diet to sculpt themselves into a so-called better version of themselves, but not Lily.

It took a while for her pride to mend, but soon she realized that Josh's problem with her size was just a cover for a problem that ran much deeper in him. And the problem, she decided, wasn't hers. It was his.

From that day forward, she decided she wasn't going to starve herself or otherwise try to change herself to fit his image of the perfect woman. She was simply going to live.

Most of all, she wasn't going to let him rob her of her belief that even at a size twelve, she was perfectly deserving of marriage and a family. Because if she ever wanted that happiness, that sense of belonging, she'd have to find it in her own family. Someday when she met the right man she would have that. Until then, she would keep doing the best she could.

"What's the matter?" Sydney asked as she came back into the room. "You look like you've seen a ghost."

In many ways Lily had. It was the ghost of her old relationship come back to haunt her. Just when she thought she'd exorcised it once and for all.

It wasn't that she wanted him back; that ship had sailed long ago. But seeing him in the paper with a woman who was everything he'd wanted her to be cut a little bit. It shouldn't, but it did.

"I wish I had brought my Spanx," Lily said as she handed the paper to Sydney, who glanced at her askance as she accepted it.

"Engagement announcements," Lily said. "Second picture in the top row."

Sydney's eyes grew wide when she obviously realized what she was looking at. "Oh! Oh, honey, I'm sorry."

"He finally found his perfect woman."

"Well, I'm sorry for her," Sydney said, in a show of solidarity that Lily simultaneously loved and hated.

Lily wasn't sorry. Or at least if she told herself that enough, she might believe it.

If the truth be told, perhaps she was sorry for herself. Sorry that everything she'd thought was real with Josh had been nothing but a mirage. How could she be with someone for that long and not see the handwriting on the wall?

They'd been together since they were teenagers and had been broken up nineteen months. Now the guy she thought was the love of her life would be married to someone else by the spring. That fast.

Badda-boom, badda-bing.

Sydney was still glowering at the paper when Lily said, "He's getting everything he ever wanted. She seems to come from a good family. She's what? A size two?"

Sydney snorted. "On a bloated day."

"I was born bigger than a size two," Lily said. She took a deep breath and exhaled. "Oh, well, I wish them nothing but the best."

"She's a sorority girl," Sydney read. "Says so right here. Tri Delta. What in the world does she want with a guy like Josh?"

"He always was ambitious," Lily said. "I guess we can't fault him for that."

"But we don't have to forgive him, either."

Lily wasn't sure if Sydney's venom stemmed from Josh's breaking Lily's heart or because he'd put Sydney in the hot seat. Her job had been in jeopardy when he'd backed out of the wedding. Sydney had pushed so hard for Lily to win the Celebration's Bride contest. Josh's decision to break the engagement had thrown the show's production into a real bind. Then, when one of the producers had wanted to use the footage of Josh breaking up with Lily in place of the wedding footage, Sydney had gone to bat to save Lily's dignity.

She was such a good friend. The source of her rancor didn't really matter.

"I'm glad you seem to be over him," Sydney said, tossing the paper aside.

"It's amazing how much a little time and distance will heal," Lily answered. If she said it out loud enough, surely she'd start to believe it. Wouldn't she?

Sydney held up a gorgeous emerald-green ball gown and cocked an eyebrow. "Of course, going to the ball with Dr. Studly does help, I'm sure."

Lily couldn't help smiling. "I think a woman would have to be dead to resist Cullen's charms."

Sydney squinted at her. "You're falling for him, aren't you?"

Lily raised her shoulders and let them fall. "Would that be such a bad thing?"

"A bad thing?" Sydney repeated. "I don't know if I'd go so far to call it a *bad thing*. Risky, maybe. I mean Cullen Dunlevy does have a reputation for dating beautiful, one-dimensional women. You certainly can hold your own in the looks category—especially in this dress." She held up the green number again and gave it a little shimmy.

"I haven't seen that side of him," Lily said. "Except for one text that he received from a woman named

Giselle. He was supposed to see her that night, but he didn't. He came home and he's been home every night since I've been working for him."

"From what I understand about Cullen, he's involved with a lot of women and none of them are interested in a relationship."

"What makes you think I'm interested in having a relationship with him?"

"Really?" Sydney gave Lily a look that said she didn't completely believe her. "You're not?"

Lily's gaze found the newspaper that Sydney had discarded. Her heart squeezed. Maybe it was just her pride. She and Josh had been together for so many years. She'd been on a few dates since they'd broken up, but she hadn't found anyone that she wanted to get serious with. Still, she knew herself well enough to know that not wanting a second date with Mr. One-Date-Wonder was a far cry from being one of many in the dating pool of a guy she wanted to see again. She couldn't deny the chemistry she felt with Cullen. Was the chemistry mutual or was that how he worked? His M.O.?

"I don't know what I want," she finally admitted.

"I don't mean to discourage you," Sydney said. "If that were the case, I wouldn't be so happy about getting Cinderella ready for the ball. I don't know Cullen well, but from what I do know, he seems different with you."

"It might be the kids," Lily said, but instantly remembered the feel of his lips on hers and the way he'd told her without mincing words that he wanted to kiss her again. Her girl parts hummed to life at the thought.

Oh, this was bad.

As if reading her mind, Sydney said, "I say go for it, but just be careful. I don't want to see you get hurt again."

Early the next morning, Lily was pulling fresh cinnamon rolls out of the oven when Cullen, who was freshly shaven, smelling like a god and all dressed and ready for work, entered the kitchen.

She'd never known simple black pants and a white button-down that was open at the collar to be quite so sexy.

"It smells like heaven in here," he said as he took a mug from the cabinet and poured himself a cup of coffee. "You do know how to tempt me, don't you?"

There was a gleam in his eye that made her stomach tingle. Maybe that was what was sexy about him. Maybe the black pants and white shirt were a blank canvas for those eyes.

"You know me," she said, holding his gaze and quirking an eyebrow. "I aim to please."

There it was.

He just made it so darn easy to flirt and she couldn't help herself. It was as if he coaxed it out of her. Yeah, but after all, he was a professional flirt. Should she expect anything else?

Full-time doctor; part-time flirt.

Or was it full-time for both? she pondered as she used a spatula to serve a steaming iced cinnamon roll.

She'd gotten to work earlier than usual, letting herself in with her door key. She'd spent a restless night tossing and turning, thinking about her conversation with Sydney. Finally she'd given in. Rather than lying there while the squirrels of doubt ran rampant in her head, she got up and went into her grandmother's kitchen that was now her kitchen and started mixing up dough for cinnamon rolls. She wasn't going to figure out anything by overthinking it. So she vowed to press on, business as usual. The rolls would have just enough time to rise and she could pop them in the oven once she got to Cullen's place. Her job was to care for the kids…and him, since he was letting her…and that was exactly what she intended to do.

Cullen was seated on the edge of a bar stool at the island, sipping his coffee and reading the paper, which Lily had brought in when she'd let herself in this morning.

That was when she noticed that he'd poured her a cup of coffee, too. It was waiting for her at the space next to him.

An invitation?

It would seem so.

Without giving it too much more thought, she set the plate in front of him and sat down on the stool next to him. She sat sideways so that she faced him.

The kids were still sleeping. The house was quiet except for the sounds of Franklin the dog, who was snoring in his bed in the corner near the window, the oven that was clicking as it cooled down and the freezer dumping a batch of freshly minted ice.

Fire and ice, she thought.

Just like the two of them: he with his hot blood; she with her cool reserve.

Little did he know that there was another side of her behind the front of capable cook and nanny.

For a moment, it felt as if they were the only two people in the world.

As he took a bite of the cinnamon roll, she sipped her coffee, holding the mug with both hands, letting the warmth seep into her palms and fingers.

"God, this is good," he said. "You made these from scratch?"

She nodded as if it were nothing.

"Do you not eat these?" he asked. "How can you not make these every day and eat them?"

"Because I'd weigh five hundred pounds if I did."

"You look perfect just the way you are," he said before he took another bite.

Perfect?

Just the way I am?

She took another sip of her coffee before she could protest. Or at least until she could think of something else to say.

"I wanted to remind you that today is a longer day at the holiday market," she said. "Do you mind if I leave the girls at the booth with Sydney and A.J. while I go pick up George from camp?"

"That's all the way on the other side of town," Cullen said. "The hospital is closer to the community center than you'll be. Why don't I just get him and bring him to you?"

"Are you sure?" she asked. "You don't mind picking him up?"

He leaned in closer, resting his arm on the back of her chair, and for a moment, she thought he was going to kiss her. And she was going to let him if he did.

But he hesitated for a moment, as if he were trying to read her or give her the chance to object. But she didn't. "I'm absolutely sure." He reached up and ran the pad of his thumb along her jawline. "In fact, I don't know when I've ever been quite so sure of anything."

Ooh. She inhaled sharply at the sensation of his touch.

Suddenly she knew he wasn't just planning on a laid-back, friendly peck, like the one they'd shared under the mistletoe at the tree lot. This was going to be the real deal, and her insides began to melt.

"Yeah?" she murmured. Her voice was barely a whisper and it sounded husky. "You sound pretty sure of yourself."

"You have no idea."

He shifted again. Their bodies were closer. Then his hand was caressing her back…. His breath was hot on her temple…. His lips skimmed her cheekbone…. She looked up at him and his eyes were hazy and hooded, and the next thing she knew, his lips were on hers, tasting like cinnamon-laced butter, black coffee and just a hint of mint…probably from his toothpaste.

He smelled so good—like soap and shave gel and something green. Lordy, she was a goner. She curled her fingers into his hair, and her senses reeled. She wanted to inhale him…devour him.

She had no idea how long they kissed, holding on to each other, lost in this moment that had been such a long time in coming. Common sense screamed that they should stop, that she should stop. She should pull away, but another part, a deeper, hungrier part, wanted to disappear into the shelter of his arms, into this place where fantasy lived and there was no such thing as mistakes or women like Giselle.

Because she wasn't like Giselle, and suddenly it was

crystal clear in her heart—as if everything had shifted and snapped into place.

Lily had fallen.

And fallen hard.

Chapter Nine

"I don't know what else to tell you, Max," Cullen said. "We're on a tight schedule. You're going to have to figure out a way to make it work. The new surgical wing has to open on time. The board refuses to give me any room for negotiations."

For a day that had started out with so much promise, it had gone straight to hell after Cullen got to work. There had been a five-car pileup on the highway that had required all hands in the emergency room, and once they'd gotten everyone stabilized, Max Cabot, the contractor who was building the new pediatric surgical wing at the hospital, had landed in his office saying that they were behind schedule on the construction. He began pushing to see if the hospital board would ease up on the clause in the contract that said the contractor would have to pay a hefty fine for each day he went over the scheduled completion date.

The board wasn't having it, and Cullen was the messenger who had to deliver the bad news.

"Look," said Max. "I'm going to confide in you. I've had a problem getting in touch with one of my subcontractors. He's MIA. That's what's holding me up."

"You're going to have to figure it out, Max. That's all I can tell you."

Before Max could protest, Cullen's administrative assistant buzzed the intercom.

"Dr. Dunlevy, Dr. Brenda Byrd is here to see you."

Brenda? Now? Great. Just what he needed. Cullen ran a hand over his eyes, trying to scrub away the irritation. This day just kept getting better and better.

He stood and walked to the office door. "Max, I'm sure you can make it work. I have faith in you."

The contractor followed, but didn't look imbued with the same confidence.

"I'll talk to you later," Max said.

Cullen gave him a curt nod and turned his attention to Brenda, who stood smiling at him as if she were the surprise guest who had just jumped out of a birthday cake. Only without the cake or the overtly sexy costume, both of which would've been much too obvious for Brenda. She'd always had her own simmering under-the-surface seductive style. But there had been so much turbulent water under the bridge that had once joined them that it had finally washed out their connection.

"Hey, Cullen," she purred. Seeing her wide smile and hearing her raspy voice took him back to the days when things had been good between them. All he could think was *I'm just not up for this right now.*

"Hello," he said. "I thought you were going to call once you got to town."

Brenda looked exactly as she always had, pretty in her sexy-smart-doctor way. Her shiny auburn hair hung in loose waves around her shoulders. She wore a silky white blouse with an expensive-looking black skirt and heels that might have been considered a little too high to be professional, but somehow she always managed to pull it off.

"I wanted to surprise you," she said.

"Mission accomplished," he said. "You did just that."

"Do you have time for coffee?" she asked.

"I have a board meeting in ten minutes." He shook his head. "It's been one of those days. Know what I mean?"

"I'm only in town for a couple days, Cullen. How about dinner tonight?"

Tonight wouldn't be enough notice for Lily.

Lily. Just the thought of her made making plans with Brenda feel like...a betrayal.

"Tonight doesn't work. You should've called me. I could've put it on my schedule."

Although a phone call wouldn't have preempted the day's chaos. He didn't want to hurt her feelings, but truth be told, he flat out didn't want to go.

"Nice to know that with notice you would've worked me in." There was an edge to her voice. She was always used to getting her way. Obviously, she still didn't like it when events didn't turn in her favor. "How about tomorrow night?"

When Cullen hesitated, she said, "I need to talk to you. I need your advice. Can you help me out? For old times' sake?"

"What's wrong?"

She let out a breath, looked around. "You have a meeting. I don't want to get into it now. Dinner tomorrow?"

When their marriage had ended, they'd prided themselves on remaining friends. Now that she might be moving to Celebration, they might very well be colleagues.

Friends made time for friends. They gave advice and all that jazz.

"I need to shuffle some things, but I'll see what I can do," he said. "I'll call you tomorrow and confirm, okay?"

"Works for me. I'll walk you to your meeting and you can start catching me up on everything that's been happening since we last spoke."

That wasn't happening now. There was too much to say to open that line of conversation before his meeting. Despite being a pediatrician, Brenda had never wanted kids of her own. That was one of the reasons their relationship had worked. Or was supposed to have worked. They were both career-focused. Medicine came first. Personal relationships followed at a close second. He thought about Lily and the kids. There was no way Brenda would understand why he'd taken in the Thomas kids. Because that meant living a kid-friendly life. It meant making yourself vulnerable and available. Like when he'd promised Lily he'd pick up George from camp—

Oh, hell. Oh, no—

"What time is it?" he asked as he pulled his cell phone out of his pocket.

Crap. It was nearly five o'clock. He was supposed to have picked up George from basketball camp at four.

That was when he saw that he had three missed calls from a number he didn't recognize on his phone, which had been on silent mode since he'd been working in the emergency room all morning.

"I have to go," he said, walking away from Brenda before he could explain.

"Where are you going? I thought you had a meeting."

"I do," he called over his shoulder. "But I have to take care of something important first. I'll call you tomorrow."

As he sprinted toward the parking lot, he pulled his cell out of his pocket and redialed the number that had called. He didn't waste time retrieving the messages. He knew what they'd say. Now he just needed to get ahold of someone who would let George know he was on his way.

"Celebration Community Center. This is April."

"Hi, April. This is Cullen Dunlevy. I'm calling about George Thomas. He's part of the holiday basketball camp. I goofed. I was supposed to pick him up at four, but I got tied up at work. I'm five minutes away. I'll be right there."

"No worries, Dr. Dunlevy. Lily Palmer just picked him up. He's safe and sound."

Cullen stopped running.

Damn.

Actually it was good that Lily had George. The poor kid must've been worried that they'd forgotten him or that something had happened. Cullen hated the thought of putting George through anything more than he'd already suffered in his young life.

"Was he…okay?"

There was a pause on the line.

"Well, honestly, he was a little upset, but he was fine once Lily arrived."

An expletive formed at the back of his throat, but he managed to swallow it.

"Thanks, April. I'm sorry. It won't happen again."

After he hung up, he stood in the parking lot debating what to do. He should go back inside. He'd be a few minutes late for the board meeting, but he wouldn't have missed anything.

Still, he couldn't make his feet move.

Instead, he dialed his assistant, Tracy. "Please give the board my apologies. I've had a family emergency and have to leave the hospital. I'll be back as soon as I can, but they should start the meeting without me."

Lily's previous irritation at Cullen for not picking up George—for not calling or returning her call—pretty much faded the minute she saw his face. He looked so guilty as he speed-walked toward the Celebrations, Inc. booth at the holiday market.

"Where's George?" he asked. "April at the community center said you picked him up. Where is he?"

Cullen looked panicked as his gaze swept the market.

"Relax," Lily said. "He and the girls are walking around and getting something to eat. He's pretty hungry."

She couldn't hide her annoyance.

"I'm sorry," he said. "I forgot."

"What do you mean *you forgot?*" Instantly she regretted her tone.

Cullen shrugged, turning his palms up as if surrendering. "I forgot. There was a bad accident on Highway 43 and they took a lot of the injured to my E.R. Then it was just one thing after another. And the next thing I knew, it was almost five o'clock. I forgot to go get him."

Dismay punched Lily in the stomach. She knew Cullen was already suffering. There was no use making him feel worse. George was safe and sound. Cullen was beyond sorry. She should've never asked Cullen to pick up the boy in the first place. It was her job. She should've just asked Sydney if she could leave the girls with her and gotten him herself. But she would never say that to Cullen.

She weighed her words. "I tried to call you. April said she tried to call you, too."

He cleared his throat. "I turned off the ringer when I was working in the emergency room and I forgot to turn it back on. I hate thinking about him sitting there waiting for me. I came straight over here to apologize to him—and you—after I learned you'd picked him up."

That was when Lily realized exactly how distraught he was over this.

She reached out and put her hand on his arm. "Hey, it's okay—"

He pulled away. "It's not okay. There's no excuse for it. I need to apologize to him before I go back to the hospital."

"Cullen, really, it's okay. Everything is fine."

"No, it's not. I promised I'd pick him up. I forgot. What kind of an idiot forgets a kid?"

"Come take a walk with me," she said to Cullen. "Do you mind if I step away for a moment, Syd?"

"Not a problem," her friend said.

They were about to take a dinner break anyway. Lily

had planned on asking Cullen to join them, but now she wasn't sure it was a good idea. "Please tell the girls and George I'll be right back."

It was becoming a familiar trek, this walk to the parking lot with Cullen.

She held the silence until they'd cleared the exit.

It was cold outside, and she pulled the collar of her jacket up around her neck. She should've thought to grab her hat.

"You said there was an emergency. You aren't used to picking up a child. Don't be so hard on yourself."

"You don't get it. I screwed up."

He braced one hand against the building's wall and raked the other through his hair. He looked like a god, standing there in the golden late-afternoon light. A tortured, brooding god. She wanted to put her arms around him until he believed everything would be okay.

"So, let me get this straight. You're calling yourself a screwup because you forgot to pick him up?"

Cullen gave a quick one-shoulder shrug.

"So, if you're a screwup for not picking him up, what does running out of gas make me?"

He glared at her.

"So, you're just going to have to forgive yourself." She closed the distance between them. "All parents slip up now and then. I'll bet ninety percent of the parents of the kids I've taught over the years have been late or even forgotten to pick up their child at least once."

She put her hand on his arm as a show of solidarity, but he shrugged it off.

"I'm *not* George's parent and I think this proves

how unfit I am to care for the kids. They deserve so much better."

"Is this discussion about what happened with George or is it because you regret kissing me this morning?"

He couldn't have looked more pain-stricken if she'd slapped him. "I don't regret kissing you, but I do think it's best that we keep our relationship platonic. It's just easier that way."

Now she was the one who felt as if she'd been slapped. "Okay. That's fine."

It wasn't fine, but what else was she supposed to say?

"I'd better go back inside." She turned around and started walking away from him. Away from every ridiculous fantasy about him turning out different from the guy her friends had warned her he was.

"Lily," he said.

She hated herself for the way her heart squeezed when he said her name. She stopped, but she didn't turn around.

"I'm sorry," he said. "I really am."

So was she. She was nearly sick with regret that Sydney, Pepper and A.J. had been right about him. He wasn't the type for anything long-term. Or maybe she simply wasn't his type.

"I need to tell you something before you go."

She turned around, careful to keep her face neutral.

"Brenda is back. She stopped by my office today."

"Who is Brenda?"

"My ex-wife."

So that was her name.

Brenda.

Brenda and Cullen.

The Drs. Dunlevy or would that be Mr. and Mrs. Dr. Dunlevy?

"Okay." The word came out flat.

She almost asked him if congratulations were in order. She thought about telling him that he was free to take Brenda to the Jingle Bell Ball, but she didn't want to sound bitter.

Damn it. She'd been looking forward to going to the ball. Now she'd have to tell Sydney that she didn't need to borrow that beautiful dress. And Sydney would get to say *I told you so.*

Nah, Sydney has too much class to do that.

But the *I told you so* would still go without saying, at least in her own head. She'd chosen, yet again, to ignore another truth.

When will you learn?

"I'm sorry," he repeated.

"Stop saying that, Cullen." This time she wasn't able to keep the edge out of her voice. "I have to go."

He nodded. "Tomorrow night, I may be a little later."

"That's not a problem," she answered coolly. "The kids and I will be working at the market. It closes at nine. After we clean up, I should have them home around ten."

"Would it be possible for you to stay a little later than that?"

Oh.

Oh, my God.

He has a date.

She stared at him, refusing to help him out of this awkward pickle. She didn't want to believe that he would actually have the audacity to ask her to babysit while he went out on a date. Not after he'd kissed her and tossed her out like yesterday's news.

He cleared his throat. "Would you be able to stay with the kids until I get home?"

Oh, and meet Brenda? That was rich. And really smooth. While she'd been sorry for him over his earlier anguish over George, it all fell away once she realized what else was on his agenda. Yes, this nanny had boundaries, and she was going to enforce them now.

"Sorry, Charlie, no can do. We'll see you when we get home at ten."

She turned and walked away.

She wasn't a femme fatale like Giselle or a world-class surgeon like Brenda.

She was simply the convenient nanny with whom Cullen had briefly contemplated hanky-panky and then run as fast as he could.

She would watch the kids during the hours they'd established because it was her job to do that, but she wasn't hanging around late into the night while he went out on a date with his ex-wife.

She burned more with each step she took, but she wasn't going to cry. There was no way she was giving him the satisfaction of that.

As she approached the booth, she took a deep breath and shoved her disappointment behind her wall.

She was such an idiot for letting things get out of hand. How could she let herself fall for him?

Well, that was then and this was now.

Things were over with Cullen and she needed to get over it.

And the first step toward that end was reminding herself that they couldn't be over when they'd never really begun.

Chapter Ten

The following night, Cullen and Brenda agreed to meet at six-thirty in the bar at Café St. Germaine before their seven o'clock dinner reservation.

They planned to have drinks before dinner and catch up on everything that had happened since their last real conversation four months ago.

Brenda was late, as usual. So Cullen grabbed a seat at the bar and ordered a Scotch and water. From where he sat, he had a great view of Main Street. The city had decorated the old gaslight-style streetlights with giant glittering stars and strung garland from lamppost to lamppost high across the road.

The storefronts had gone all out with their holiday window displays. On a Roll Bakery was even featuring loaves of Lily's homemade stollen in the window.

Lily.

She was everywhere.

Everywhere he looked he saw something that reminded him of her: her bread in the window; the farmers' market (he'd passed it on the way to Café St. Germaine); the athletic-shoe shop where she'd tried to take George to get his shoes before she ran out of gas. He harrumphed to himself when he recalled how she'd turned the tables on him when he was brooding over forgetting to pick up the boy.

He wasn't excusing himself, but she was right. He knew he hadn't purposely left the kid any more than she'd purposely run out of gas on the way to Dallas. None of the women he'd dated had been as forthright as Lily. Well, except for Brenda, and he'd married her.

However, what Lily had that Brenda lacked—and Brenda had many fine attributes: she was intelligent, beautiful and driven—was heart. Lily had a huge heart, always thinking of others, often before herself.

Sure, Lily challenged him at times—she certainly had a smart mouth to go along with that big heart. But it was her compassion that set her apart from the rest.

A pang of regret twisted in his gut. He felt like a bastard for treating her the way he had yesterday. It was the only way he could make the emotional break from her. He was damn lucky that *she* hadn't insisted on a clean break and left him and the kids high and dry to fend for themselves.

He would've deserved it—the same way he deserved the cool greeting he'd received when she brought the kids home after the first long night at the holiday market. He'd also deserved the sleepless night that had him tossing and turning into the wee hours of the morning, thinking about what a jackass he'd been to kiss her and cut her loose. But she and the kids, they were just getting too close...

He hated that about himself, that need to push people away when they got too close. That was the one thing he'd change if he could, but he was powerless. It was like asking an elephant to downsize. He certainly wasn't proud of this disconnect, but he didn't know how to change.

The kids would be so much better off with two adoptive parents who would welcome them as part of their family. But he kept circling back to the reality that so far Cam Brady hadn't had any luck finding a family that wanted to adopt four kids. With each passing day, hopes of that happening before the end of the year grew dimmer and slimmer.

Thank God for Lily. He'd been grateful when she'd arrived right on schedule. She'd quietly busied herself while he'd poured himself a travel mug of coffee. But there'd been no fresh-baked cinnamon rolls, none of the personal niceties that she'd gone out of her way to provide in the past. He had definitely been left to fend for himself, and he deserved it.

As Cullen took a long draw on his Scotch, Jake Lenox, an internist at Celebration Memorial, walked in with his girlfriend of the moment, a leggy brunette his coworkers had nicknamed Miss Texas. Jake was proudly showing her off like the trophy she was, but Cullen had to wonder if Jake was really happy.

Of course, on the surface, who wouldn't be happy to be with such a beautiful woman? Miss Texas was one of several beauties who had been in Jake's life over the years. The guy tended to be a serial monogamist. But

Miss Texas had been around longer than some of the others. Was his friend actually getting serious?

Cullen knew he was guilty of similar romantic crimes. While Jake dated one woman for a few months before moving on, Cullen had an endless revolving door of short-term beautiful women. Funny how that door had stopped revolving once Lily and the kids had arrived. Had he given Lily the brush-off yesterday so he could reopen that sad process? Honestly, it didn't even seem appealing right now. In fact, it felt like going backward.

Since he didn't know what he wanted right now, it was best not to do anything.

Jake waved at Cullen and steered Miss Texas toward that end of the bar. Cullen knocked back the last of his Scotch.

"Hey, buddy, are you alone?" Jake asked.

"I'm waiting for someone."

"Let me buy you a drink while you wait," said Jake. "Have you met Dorenda?"

"Yes, we met at Quinn Vogler's Labor Day party."

Dorenda simpered and offered Cullen her cheek. As any gentleman would, he kissed her. In the process he nearly choked on her perfume and almost lost an eye compliments of a shellacked curl.

Jake left the two of them alone while he ordered the drinks.

"Have you eaten here before?" Cullen asked.

"No," she said. "I'm from Dallas."

"What do you do in Dallas?"

"I'm a model."

Not really in the mood for small talk, Cullen glanced at his watch. Was Brenda standing him up?

Order placed, Jake rejoined the party and started

talking shop. Forty-five minutes later, while Cullen was halfway through drinks with Jake, Brenda finally arrived.

"So sorry I'm late. I had to go back to the hotel and freshen up. I spent the whole day at Celebration Pediatrics. Looks like it could be a good fit. Although, if I do come on board, several things will have to change."

Typical Brenda. No call. No text. It was still all about her. Cullen managed to commandeer the conversation long enough to introduce Brenda to his friends.

"I'm sorry. I don't think I caught your last name," he said to Dorenda.

"Parks," she said. "Dorenda Parks."

"Dorenda Parks, this is Brenda Byrd. Brenda, this is Dorenda."

"Dorenda and Brenda," Jake said. "You're practically twins."

Brenda eyed Miss Texas dubiously. "Nice to meet you." Her tone was cool.

"What would you like to drink, Brenda?" Jake asked.

"Nothing, thanks. I'm sure Cullen is starving. Why don't we go see if our table is ready?"

"She gets cranky when she's hungry," Cullen tried to joke, hoping to cover for her brusqueness.

"I'm not cranky," she said. "I was only thinking of you."

This was going nowhere fast. "I think we'd better go see if they're still holding our reservation."

Brenda was busy checking her phone and didn't seem to hear Cullen's attempt to cover for her aloofness. Or maybe she did and just didn't care. That was entirely possible. This detachment had been a factor in why they had divorced. She was a hell of a doctor, but she still lacked charm and bedside manner unless she chose to turn it on.

Since they were so late, they'd lost the reservation, but after Cullen primed the hostess with a twenty, she remembered she had a table in the back and seated them immediately.

"How did your emergency turn out yesterday?" Brenda asked once they were settled at the table.

Cullen glanced at her over the top of the wine list. "Everything is fine. Do you want red or white?" Everything wasn't fine, but he didn't want to talk about it.

"I don't know. It will depend on what I order."

The server came with a basket of bread and took their drink orders—chardonnay for Brenda, merlot for him. She promised to take their dinner order when she returned.

"Actually I need to be home by ten," Cullen said.

"Curfew?" She smiled and arched a brow before she sipped her water.

"Babysitter."

She choked and then wiped the corners of her mouth with her napkin.

"Excuse me? Did you say *babysitter?*"

"I did. Although she's more of a nanny than a babysitter, and the kids would take issue with me saying they were being babysat."

Brenda leaned forward, her jaw slack. "Whoa. Whoa, back up. Kids. As in plural? Who are old enough to object to being babysat?"

She narrowed her eyes. "Oh, okay. I get it. You're joking, aren't you? Very funny, Cullen. You almost had me there."

"I'm not joking, Brenda." He raised his right hand.

"Honest. I have four kids, ages five to ten, living with me."

"But they're not yours," she said. "You couldn't have a ten-year-old. We were married then."

It was a strange feeling the way he wanted to object to her statement that they weren't his. "Obviously we have a lot of catching up to do," Brenda said. "Where did these kids come from?"

Cullen picked up his water glass and took a sip. "Do you remember when I introduced you to Greg Thomas, my best friend growing up?"

She looked up from the menu. "Oh, right. He and his wife came to visit right after you and I started dating. They drove that little blue convertible."

"Yes, he's the one."

He told her about Greg's accident, how he'd promised Megan she could call him if she and her siblings ever needed anything, and how she'd held him to that promise when the adoptive family Greg and Rosa had secured fell through.

"I'm sorry, Cullen. I know Greg was a good friend. That must've been difficult for you. But I have to say, four kids? What are you going to do?"

Cullen shook his head. "I'm trying to figure it out, but right now I just don't see any other choice but to find them a family that will adopt them. I have a family-law attorney working on it. I won't let them be split up. I refuse to let them get swept up by the foster-care system."

"You do realize how difficult it will be to keep four kids together? That's going to be tricky. What are you going to do if you can't find someone to take them all?"

"I'll cross that bridge if and when I come to it."

"Don't tell me you're thinking about keeping them,

because you need four kids like you need a hole in the head."

He closed his menu. "Brenda, you haven't met them. They're pretty cool. They're smart and fun. They keep me and Lily on our toes."

Like yesterday, when he forgot George. Common sense reminded him that there was being challenged, and then there was being in denial. Denial to the point that he was ignoring what was best for the kids.

Then, as if she were reading his mind, she said, "Is Lily the nanny, or is she someone special?"

"She's very special."

He surprised himself when the thought morphed into words.

"Oh, I see." She sounded disappointed. Her gaze searched his eyes, and he could see the wheels in her head turning.

Before he could clarify, she said, "Cullen, you do realize that basically you gave up your right to a normal family life when you took the Hippocratic oath? You're married to your job. You'd need a live-in nanny if you adopted four kids. So don't make me come over there and smack some sense into you."

She smiled at him as if she had just made a joke, but he could tell by her body language that there was at least some grain of seriousness to it. That was the thing about Brenda: she had honed passive aggression into an art form.

Still, her words echoed in his head and gave him pause.

You gave up your right to a normal family life.

"Didn't you ask me to dinner because you wanted my advice? I seem to remember you saying that."

"Yes. Yes. I want to know everything you can tell me about working and living in Celebration. But— Look, I didn't mean to sound like I was telling you what to do. I simply hate to see you make a mistake that might end up leaving these children worse off than they are now."

They sat in uncomfortable silence for a moment.

And she reached out and put her hand on top of his.

"I'll be honest. Sometimes I think leaving you was the biggest mistake I ever made in my life," she said. "The last few months, I found myself thinking about you a lot. About us. Then when I learned of the possibility of the job right here in Celebration, I thought it had to be a sign. And you know me. I don't believe in signs."

What? Oh, no. They'd been there, done that, and they'd learned that the two of them were great as friends and colleagues, but terrible as a couple.

"Now that we're settled in our careers and we've both been around the block a bit, maybe we could try again? I mean, we could take things slowly. *If* I end up taking the job here."

He suddenly felt a little claustrophobic, as if the walls were closing in. So, this was what she wanted to pick his brain about. Living and working in Celebration with him—a minor detail that she'd forgotten to mention.

"Don't take the Celebration Pediatrics job for me— or for us. You need to go through with the other interviews you have lined up and not make any decisions until you can compare offers and choose the one that's best for you."

She lifted her chin.

"Of course," she said, but he could see the disappointment in her eyes. "It's the sensible thing to do. Your saying that is case in point of why we would be so good together. We understand each other so well."

Funny thing was, Cullen didn't understand her at all. Never had, never would.

Cullen's phone rang, and he fished it out of his pocket, wanting to see not only who was calling but the time. His gut tightened when he saw Lily's name and number on the display.

He stood. "Excuse me. I need to take this."

He answered as he walked toward the restrooms.

"Hi, Lily. Is everything okay?"

"Hi. I'm so sorry to bother you, but Bridget is running a fever. I brought her and the kids home early from the holiday market because she was just feeling lousy. I was going to wait until you got home to ask you about ibuprofen, but there's no need for her to suffer like this when I can just give you a quick call."

"You did the right thing. How high is her fever?"

Lily told him and Cullen gave her instructions and said he would be home as soon as he could.

"I'm so sorry to ruin your night. You really don't have to come home now. I'm sure she'll be fine."

"It's okay. We were just wrapping things up anyway."

He took care of the check before he returned to the table, wanting to avoid an awkward struggle over Brenda's insistence on splitting the bill.

Once he got back to the table, he said, "I'm so sorry to do this, but I have to go. That was Lily, and one of the girls is sick. I really should go and check in on her."

Something flashed in Brenda's eyes.

"Since we'll virtually pass your house on the way

to my hotel, why don't I go with you and look in on the child? After all, I am a pediatrician. Usually I don't make house calls, but for you I'll make an exception."

Chapter Eleven

Lily was surprised that Cullen had been so eager to come home. She had warred with herself over whether to call but finally gave in to good sense.

This was about Bridget, not about them. Her concern was for the girl. If he wanted to take it upon himself to come home, that was his decision.

As she sat in the chair next to Bridget's bed, she refused to let herself be nervous about seeing him. She also refused to let her mind wander over the reasons that he might have been willing to cut this date short. Sure, she had told him she needed to leave by ten o'clock, but she hadn't expected him to sound eager to be home early.

When she heard footsteps in the hallway she decided to stay seated.

Bridget was dozing, the ibuprofen finally kicking

in, and the children were in the family room watching television. George and Hannah hadn't balked when Lily put Megan in charge. Of course, the big bowl of popcorn and the movie of their choice put them in a cooperative mood, but they'd also been subdued by the fact that their sister was under the weather.

After they'd lost their parents, it had to be scary when anything was wrong with one of the four of them. How Lily wished she could promise them with 100 percent certainty that everything from this point out would be okay. But she couldn't read the future. It broke her heart, but she had no idea where the sweet kids would end up after the first of the year. The only thing she could do now was to be there for them and give them the best Christmas they could hope for.

When Cullen entered the room, Lily was ready to apologize again for taking him away from his dinner, but then she realized he wasn't alone.

Her heart plummeted when she saw the beautiful woman at his side. She knew it was Brenda before the woman introduced yourself.

"You must be Lily. I've heard so much about you."

Maybe Lily was imagining it, but Brenda's smile didn't seem completely sincere. It made Lily wonder— had they been talking about her?

Reruns of yesterday's conversation with Cullen played through her head. While she didn't think he was the type to talk badly about someone, she couldn't help worrying about what he might have told Brenda. Still, since she didn't have any control over that, she couldn't let herself focus on it.

If she tallied up all of her inadequacies—because Josh had given her a laundry list of every single one of her shortcomings when he broke up with her and they were still very fresh in her mind—she could very well let them get the best of her.

She wasn't going to do that. So what if Brenda was intimidatingly beautiful and a doctor to boot? Lily was who she was and she wasn't going to make any apologies for that.

"You must be Brenda." Lily mustered her most genuine smile. "It's so nice to meet you."

"Brenda is a pediatrician," Cullen said. "She's going to look in on Bridget."

"That's wonderful of you," she said. Although, she hated for her to wake up Bridget. There was no telling how long it would take the girl to get back to sleep. But Brenda was the pediatrician. She knew what was best. With a heavy heart for the sick girl and, yes, she had to admit, a little for herself, too, Lily knew it would be best to say good-night.

"Now that I know Bridget's in good hands, I'll say good-night and go home. Cullen, why don't I take Megan, George and Hannah home with me? You'll have your hands full with Bridget tonight."

And if Dr. Perfect decided to stay the night—to look in on the sick girl, of course—it would definitely be a full house with all of them there. Lily just hoped to God that the woman was gone before she dropped the kids off in the morning.

Or would she be dropping them off in the morning? Things had been so hectic and strange that she and Cullen hadn't even had a chance to discuss the weekend schedule. Maybe he was expecting her to take the kids to the holiday market. She planned on being there to help out anyway. She might as well take the kids directly there.

Great. And leave the day wide-open with the two to rekindle the romance. Of course, someone would need to stay with the sick girl—

"I can't ask you to do that," he said. "You've already had a long day."

Brenda threw them a look over her shoulder as she was checking Bridget's vitals.

"Let's go out in the hall so that we don't disturb Brenda," Lily suggested.

Cullen shut the bedroom door behind him and the two of them were alone in the hall. Lily could hear the faint sound of the movie the kids were watching. One of the girls, probably Hannah, giggled at something funny. Lily wished she were down there with them. Actually she wished she were any place other than where she was right now—standing face-to-face with this man who had broken her heart.

"You seem upset," Cullen said.

Well, yes...

"I'm just worried about Bridget. Like you said, it's been a long day."

"Please stay," he said. His face looked anguished.

Lily blinked. Just a moment ago he had been acknowledging how tired she must be. Now he was asking her to stay?

Her chest felt tight and her words were having a hard time getting past the lump in her throat. Oh, dear God, please let her keep her composure. The last thing she needed to do right now was lose it in front of this man who had made her place in his life perfectly clear yesterday. What made it even worse was that his ex-wife was in the next room.

No. Just no.

He'd set his boundaries yesterday. Tonight she would set hers.

"Cullen, I'm happy for the kids to come home with me, but I need to leave. I'm going to go tell them to get their stuff ready. Maybe Brenda will stay and help you with Bridget."

She turned toward the stairs.

"She's going to be leaving in a few minutes. Please stay.... I need you."

Lily paused at the top of the stairs. She turned and looked at him. The way he was looking at her made her want to believe he really did *need* her. But she had to keep it in context. He had made himself perfectly clear yesterday.

Still, she couldn't stop herself from saying, "Don't. Cullen, please. Don't."

"I made a mistake yesterday."

Oh, no. She felt the tears welling in her eyes. She reached up to swipe them away before they could take on a life of their own. "How was your date?"

"Let's just say that it was a dinner between old friends."

Lily gave him a look.

"That's all we are. All she and I will ever be."

A hiccuping sob escaped Lily as a tear crested and rolled down her cheek. Cullen reached up and brushed it away.

"I'm sorry," he said. "I'm so sorry."

Brenda cleared her throat. She was standing in the hallway watching them. "Well, it appears to be a virus.

She should be fine in a day or so. I think my work here is done. I guess I'll go wash my hands."

"Brenda, please let me drive you back to your hotel," Cullen said as he and his ex-wife stood face-to-face in the upstairs hall. Before Brenda had emerged from the bathroom after washing her hands, Lily had excused herself to go downstairs with the other three kids. Bridget was sound asleep and they were both visibly relieved that her prognosis was good.

"Don't be ridiculous." Her voice was eerily calm. "I've already called a cab. It should be here any minute. But please do come wait with me outside until it arrives."

It was the least he could do. He wasn't going to let her stand out there alone or awkwardly in the foyer waiting for her ride.

She buttoned up her coat and twisted her scarf into place. Cullen shrugged into his jacket and they stepped into the cold night air.

They stood a respectable distance apart and were silent for a moment. He could virtually hear the wheels turning in her mind.

"Lily is a beautiful woman. She seems to genuinely care for the children."

"She's a second-grade teacher. She's great with kids. I was lucky to find her."

Brenda made a skeptical noise, half laugh, half derision.

"To care for the children, I mean," he clarified.

Brenda sighed and gave a dismissive wave of her hand. "Some women are cut out for motherhood. I'm not. That's just how I'm wired. I can deal with sick children, but I'm always happy to give them back to the parents."

Cullen shoved his hands deeper into his coat pockets. It was so cold he wouldn't be surprised if it snowed tonight. "Can I ask you a question?"

"Sure. Ask me anything."

There was a note of resignation in her voice, as if she were willing to play along but didn't expect much.

"Why did you become a pediatrician if you're not fond of children? Never could figure that out about you."

She snorted. "One of the many mysteries of me. Let me say this—I don't think it's strange that you don't necessarily want to live with your patients."

"Touché."

The cab pulled into the driveway. Brenda paused before she got into the car. "You know she's in love with you. It's written all over her face. I think you're in love with her, too. Am I right?"

"Good night, Brenda," he said.

She laughed again, though it sounded humorless. "Goodbye, Cullen."

He stood there for a moment watching the cab's taillights grow smaller as it carried her away. As the car disappeared into the night, he felt a weight that he hadn't even realized he'd been carrying vanish with it.

When he got back inside, Lily was in the kitchen finishing up what he guessed were the dinner dishes.

"It's late," he said. "Don't worry about those."

"I only have a few more left to do. It's not a problem, really. I got the kids to bed while you were outside."

He walked over and turned off the water she had

running in the sink to rinse the dishes. She looked up at him, a startled expression on her beautiful face.

He looked at her, searched every inch of her face, needing to verify what Brenda saw. He needed to see it for himself, because he knew what he was feeling. He was in love with Lily Palmer, despite how he'd tried to drive her away, hoping that she would take the strange feeling that had been growing in him with her when she went.

His whole life, everybody he'd ever loved had left him. His dad had never wanted to stick around; his mother had died; Brenda had left him—had left their marriage—and when she left she had taken all his feelings, his entire capacity to love, with her. In a strange way, it was as if she returned everything she had taken.

Now, if he hadn't already blown it, he knew exactly who owned his heart. "Will you forgive an idiot?"

She looked at him as if he were crazy. And he was. Crazy for her. Crazy for letting her go. "Can you be more specific?"

"Let's just say it took dinner with my ex-wife to help me realize exactly what I was losing."

Lily blanched.

For the love of God, could he make this sound any worse?

"Brenda came back to Celebration with her mind set on us reconciling. But we both realized tonight that my heart isn't available."

Lily frowned at him. He could see her wall going up again, as she opened her mouth to say something.

"It's not available to her because it belongs to you. If you'll have it. Please tell me you will. Or feel free to tell me I'm a fool. And you can walk away. I wouldn't blame you if you did. Yesterday, forgetting George brought up some personal issues that I'll have to tell you about sometime. It triggered some bad memories. That, mixed with Brenda's surprise appearance and realizing that I'm in love with you. I just— I didn't handle it very well."

Her hand flew to her mouth, and she watched the carefully erected wall she'd built around herself fall, brick by brick.

The next thing Lily knew, she was in his arms and his lips were on hers. It started as a featherlight kiss and it made her heart pound and her brain fog as reason flew out the window.

It began easy and slow—a brush of lips and hints of tongue, testing the waters. So she slid her arms around his neck, her hands into his hair, and opened her mouth, inviting him in.

Cullen's hands were on her back, and his mouth was on her lips, and all her girl parts sang, *Oooh, yes, please,* as every sense was heightened by his touch.

He deepened the kiss a few layers. Her whirling mind registered her pounding heart and the velvet feel of his lips on hers—skilled lips, capable hands… Losing herself in that kiss, in him, she enjoyed how he made her feel…so alive and…wanton…craving his touch…his lips on her temple, her earlobe, her neck—

The feel of him teased her senses, making her feel hot and sexy and just a little bit reckless—

She pulled back, gasping for air, more than a little bit disoriented. Fearing she was going to wake up from this lovely dream to find herself cold and alone—or worse yet, that they would look over and discover that they had an audience of four, or three, since sweet Bridget was sick. But even if one child caught them—

"Cullen, I'm there. I'm so there," she said, but she hesitated. She wasn't going to put up with this back-and-forth nonsense. "But maybe we need to talk about exactly where it is we're going. You can see that it takes every ounce of everything I have to resist you."

A low moan escaped his throat and he looked at her as if he didn't plan on giving her any help in the abstinence department.

And that was fine. She didn't want *abstinence,* but she did want to make sure they wanted the same things and went about them the right way.

"I can't stay with you tonight," she said. "Not with the kids in the house. How would we explain that? It would be too confusing, and God knows they don't need any more confusion in their lives."

He nodded. "You're right. You're absolutely right."

She held up her hand, trying to ignore the way her lips felt swollen and wanting and her intimate parts were ready to mutiny and say to hell with propriety. So she bit down on her bottom lip to help her think straight. "I need to know that what happened yesterday isn't going to happen again—"

"I swear to you. I just needed to sort out everything. And I did."

"And I'm glad," she said. "So, this week we're going to take things slowly. We'll know when the time is right."

Possibly the Jingle Bell Ball next Saturday?

Chapter Twelve

Now, gazing at her across the crowded dance floor of the Grand Puerto Vallarta Hotel, she'd looked as if she'd stepped from a dream—his own recurring dream that had been playing on an endless loop since he came to his senses last week. Cullen felt a stir of desire as he returned to Lily with two flutes of champagne.

Her emerald-green gown hugged those perfect curves. She looked soft and sensual and so damn sexy that his groin tightened with appreciation. Since she'd come into his life three weeks ago—had it been only three weeks?—he couldn't remember his life without her. It had been love at first sight, whether he wanted to believe it or not. But the truth of the matter remained. The moment he'd first set eyes on her something inside him had shifted; life as he knew it had ceased to exist once she had arrived. Life had gone from shades of gray and going-through-the-motions to days and nights filled with purpose and breathtaking possibility.

The orchestra transitioned into the beginning strains of "Can't Take My Eyes Off You." When he reached the table, he set down the champagne and held out his hand. "Dance with me."

"I thought you'd never ask."

On the dance floor, he swept her into his arms. She gazed up at him, her eyes dark green and full of emotion. Their lips were a breath apart as they swayed together— not in a formal dance that moved them around the room, but in a slow, private dance that moved through them, joining them, making them one.

Since last week, he hadn't looked back, and now that she was in his arms, he intended to keep moving forward—as fast as she would let him.

He took a deep breath, losing himself in the scent of her. He wouldn't let himself overthink it. He would just go with it.

The dance floor was crowded, but it was nice holding her in his arms. They danced to three more songs before Lily suggested, "How about we drink that champagne now?"

He stepped back to lead her off the dance floor, but she was frozen in place, staring at a man dancing with a blonde a few couples over from them. The guy, who was staring back at her, seemed just as surprised to see her.

"Is everything all right?" Cullen asked.

Lily leaned in and whispered, "That's Josh." By this time, the guy had maneuvered his date so that they were dancing next to them.

"Lily." The guy leaned in and planted a kiss on her,

a little too close to her lips for Cullen's liking. "I didn't expect to see you here."

Cullen didn't appreciate the way he was looking at Lily.

"Well, surprise. Here I am. I didn't expect to see you, either. Cullen, this is Josh Stockett." She smiled, but Cullen could read between the lines. It took him a moment before he put a name with the face and realized this was her ex-fiancé. "Josh, my date, Cullen Dunlevy."

Cullen offered his hand. Josh gave a perfunctory shake, and Cullen picked up on the tension.

Josh's full attention was on Lily.

"How have you been?" he asked.

"I've never been better," she said.

"Hi, Lily," Josh's date said, inserting herself into the conversation. "I'm Ann-Elizabeth Hardy, soon to be Ann-Elizabeth Stockett." The woman giggled and flashed a diamond solitaire on her left hand. "Josh and I are getting married. How do you and Josh know each other?"

How do we know each other?

Had the jackass not told her he'd been engaged? She slanted a look at Josh, who looked as though he was holding his breath.

It would be fun to torture him or introduce herself as the former future Mrs. Josh Stockett. But the guy wasn't worth it.

"Oh, Josh and I? We go way back."

"We sure do," said Josh. "In fact, how about a dance for old times' sake?"

Lily looked at Cullen, hoping he would intervene. But he was no help.

"By all means," he said. "Be my guest. In fact, Ann-Elizabeth, would you do me the honor?"

Traitor!

The orchestra was playing a jazzy version of "Fly Me to the Moon." Josh slipped his arm around Lily's waist. She put her left hand in his, in the obligatory formal dance position. The guy couldn't dance, but he was pretending to.

Lily was damned if she was going to be the one to start the conversation. So they moved in awkward fashion in the opposite direction of where Cullen and Ann-Elizabeth were dancing.

She wasn't about to address the elephant between them, the fact that he hadn't bothered to tell the woman he was going to marry that he'd almost married someone else. Wasn't that just so Josh Stockett?

"How have you been?" he finally said.

"You already asked me that, Josh. And I said I've never been better."

"Cullen seems like a nice guy."

That was a layup. A chance to go on about how Cullen was a man who knew how to talk about his feelings, didn't ignore the things that were hard to talk about until he was backed into a corner and a camera was rolling to capture the whole thing on film. But there was no sense in rehashing it tonight on the dance floor at the Jingle Bell Ball.

Josh had already proved he had a talent for leaving Lily to discuss the good and important things. She wasn't going to let Josh taint this night.

So, digging deep into her Southern manners, she said, "He's such a great guy."

"Thank you for being cool with Ann-Elizabeth."

"Cool? I don't know what you mean."

"Obviously I haven't told her about us."

Us?

Hearing the word used in that context made Lily feel a little sick and grateful they were no longer an *us*.

"You might want to do that," Lily said. "Maybe not tonight…. Or you know what, on second thought, maybe you should do it tonight. You owe it to her, Josh. You owe it to the woman you're going to marry to be honest with her even if it's a hard conversation. Because if the relationship can't survive honesty, it's doomed from the start."

Josh blanched. They danced without talking for several moments. When the song was over, Lily turned to leave, but Josh held on to her hand.

"I'm sorry," he said. "You deserve to be treated a lot better than I treated you, and I want to apologize. That's me being honest with you."

She weighed his words for a moment, but all she could find in them was sincerity. "Thank you, Josh. Ann-Elizabeth seems like a nice girl. Good luck to the two of you. I hope you'll treat her right."

He smiled as he let go of her hand and she turned and walked away.

Cullen was waiting for her on the edge of the dance floor.

"Whose side are you on?" she whispered when she reached him.

"Your side, of course." He smiled a knowing smile. "It's important to take care of unfinished business."

Lily shrugged.

"Closure is important," he said. "Take it from someone who knows. Because you can't move on until you settled your past."

"Spoken like a man who knows what he's talking about."

Cullen nodded. "Are you ready to move on?"

There was more to that question than face value suggested. Lily took a moment before answering to search her heart. Was she ready to move on?

There were different reasons that a person might stay stuck in the past. You could harbor hopes of getting back together and miss out on life while holding out for a chance to be reunited.

She could also hold out because she was deluding herself, which was what she'd been doing with Josh.

She didn't want him.

No. No, she didn't. Ann-Elizabeth, bless her heart, could have him. Lily just hoped that Josh was honest with her and didn't put her through the same misery he'd put her through. "You have no idea just how ready I am," she said.

Cullen leaned in and kissed her. His lips lingered long enough to entice her to lean in for more, as he ran a strong hand up her back.

When they broke apart, she saw Josh standing there watching her with a look on his face that suggested he wasn't entirely happy witnessing the scene. Poor Ann-Elizabeth, Josh's perfect debutante, was watching her beloved fiancé watch Lily, with an uncertain look that Lily was all too familiar with.

"Come on. Let's get out of here," Lily said, feeling free and cleansed of Josh for the first time since he'd broken her heart.

Cullen put his arm around her and pulled her in close as they walked out of the ballroom.

They didn't talk on the way back to Cullen's house. Yet it was an emotionally charged silence. They both knew what was going to happen when they got home. The girls were staying at Sydney's, and George was at a sleepover at the home of one of Cullen's colleagues who had a son George's age. The boys had become fast friends after Lily had invited the boy over for a play-date. It was like a breath of fresh air to see George so happy after the basketball-camp fiasco.

It was just the two of them tonight. It was the first time they'd been alone for any significant amount of time without having to worry that the kids were going to pop in.

God knew they couldn't keep their hands off each other when they were pressed for time.

So, yeah, they knew what would happen next. It was as inevitable as the sun rising in the east that she'd wake up in his bed tomorrow morning.

Knowing that—and they both knew it—the twenty-minute drive from Dallas back to Celebration could've been a cooling-off period for either of them. A chance to realize this was a mistake. But it wasn't.

Lily refused to allow words—small talk, or big important declarations of love, or lack thereof—to talk them out of what had been inevitable since the first time they'd laid eyes on each other.

When Cullen put his hand on her knee and sensually slid it up—higher, higher—and when he would lean over and plant kisses on her lips at a stoplight and trail kisses down her neck at stop signs, she knew he, too, refused to let words get in the way.

The silence broken only by the kisses and the feel of his hand, which had found its way under her gown and had taken possession of her thigh, heightened the anticipation of what was to come.

Finally he steered the car into the driveway and they were alone in the house. Just the two of them. In the foyer, it was silent except for the distant strains of the Christmas carols playing on the radio that they always left on these days. The large wooden front door was the only thing between them and the outside world.

They stood together. His lips were a mere fraction from hers. He was so close that they were breathing the same air. She could smell the intoxicating scent of him—he smelled like heaven: a subtle blend of soap and grassy aftershave mixed with an indefinable masculine note that was all him. The essence of him had infused itself on her senses and it had gone to her head faster than the champagne they'd enjoyed tonight. She was still tipsy from the champagne and the freedom of bidding Josh a final farewell, but she was drunk on Cullen—his taste, his scent, the way she imagined his body would feel on hers.

She wasn't sure who moved first, but suddenly they were in each other's arms. In one heated motion, he'd pulled her into his embrace and backed her against the door, kissing her all the while. Just as he had possession of her body, he'd stolen her heart. She wanted to tell him he could have them. Both of them. They already belonged to him, but she did not have to say it.

He understood.

He laced his fingers through hers and pressed their

bodies together. She felt him respond to her as parts of him swelled and hardened. The feel of him sent heat thrumming through her. The simple sensation of his mouth on hers swept her away into a world that was theirs alone. The past couldn't touch them and the future seemed a million miles away.

Things between them were different now. Or maybe it had always been this way, but right now, in this moment, this *thing* that had been brewing between them felt deeper and impossibly right.

For the first time in a long while, Lily's guard dropped and her heart opened to possibility.

He let go of her hands and wrapped himself around her, shifting his body to deepen the kiss. Her hands explored the expanse of his shoulders, trailed down the hard muscles of his back.

His kisses sent spirals of ecstasy unfurling in her belly. That shimmer of heat sparked and yearning flamed and burned deep and hot. She couldn't remember when she'd wanted a man as much as she wanted him. The thought of making love to him right there in the foyer sent a hungry shudder through her whole body. Suddenly she needed him naked and on top of her so that he could bury himself inside her.

Now.

Right now.

But Cullen had different plans. He led her out of the foyer. At the base of the stairs, he scooped her up and kissed her deeply as they made their way upstairs.

The journey to his bedroom was the longest path she'd ever traveled, longer than the car ride home, longer than it had taken them to arrive at this moment.

When they finally reached his room, he set her down

and they stumbled through the doorway, pulling at each other's clothes, driven only by the burning need to get closer, closer, until their bodies joined as one.

Somewhere between the car and the bedroom, he had lost his tie, and the first couple of buttons of his shirt were undone.

As tongues thrust and hands explored, she was vaguely aware of him unzipping her dress. She shrugged out of it, letting it fall to the floor, leaving her in her panties, thigh-high stockings and the high heels she had worn with the dress.

He inhaled sharply and moaned at the sight of her standing there. He held her away from him and looked at her for one reverent moment.

Then his hands were on her breasts and a little moan of pleasure escaped her own lips. His touch was possessive. She wanted him to possess her. Every single inch of her.

She unbuttoned a few more buttons on his shirt and pulled it over his head, wanting skin on skin. Wanting to touch and be touched. Wanting his hands on her body in places that had ached for him since the first moment she'd seen him. His hands slid down her bare back and cupped her bottom through her panties, pulling her to him.

As her body begged for the hardness of him to find its way home, she reached out, unbuttoned his pants and slid down the zipper. He moved to free himself of his clothes.

It had been a long time since she'd allowed herself to fully want, to fully trust, to be *this* vulnerable, but all that mattered now was how much she needed him.

Because his need for her was evident and it made her feel powerful and beautiful. Strong and desirable.

He wanted her exactly the way she was.

No man had ever made her feel this beautiful before.

After the rest of her clothes had fallen away, he walked her backward to the bed and laid her down, covering her with his body.

"Are you okay?" he asked, his lips still brushing hers, ever so slightly. Those were the first words either of them had uttered since leaving the ball.

"You have no idea just how okay I am right now." Her voice sounded raspy as she wrapped her arms around him. She reveled at how his broad back narrowed at the waist and at the sheer masculine width and breadth of him.

In turn, he smoothed a wisp of hair off her forehead and kissed the skin he'd just uncovered with such tenderness it nearly made her cry. He searched her eyes. She answered him with a kiss that promised, *Yes, I want this. I want you.*

She longed to tell him exactly how many different ways she had imagined this moment and how glad she was that they no longer had to deny themselves.

But that would take too many words.

Tonight was not a night of words. And that was a good thing because the words couldn't find their way past her lips.

Still, he answered her silently with a sultry smile as he reached over, pulled open the drawer to his bedside table and took out a few condoms, which he tossed on top of the nightstand, where they would be ready and waiting when they needed them.

Once again, just as he'd done in the foyer, his hands

found hers, and he laced their fingers together. She looked at their entwined hands. His were big and handsome, masculine hands. They lingered a moment on hers, gripping, flexing, hesitating, as if he were silently giving her one last chance to change her mind, to flee, back to just friends. After knowing each other for three weeks, they'd left behind the pretense of boss and nanny.

And there was no turning back now. That was the last thing she wanted.

A rush of red-hot need spiraled through her. He must have read it in her face, because he let go of her hands, and in a fevered rush, he rolled over onto his back, bringing her with him. As he kissed her softly, gently, her fingers found their way into his hair. She pulled him close, closer, until they were kissing with an all-consuming need.

His warm palms slipped between them and splayed over her breasts. His fingers paid reverence to her nipples, then trailed down her belly, where they lingered and played, tracing small circles that made her stomach muscles tighten and spasm in such agonizing pleasure that all her girl parts sang.

Actually they weren't singing. They were begging.

Then his hand slid even farther still, teasing its way toward her center, toward a hidden silken place that had been craving his touch.

But after another swift move, she found herself underneath him again. Her fingers swept over his tight shoulders and muscled arms, exploring the firm sinew before going south and discovering the curve of his tight derriere. She pulled him closer, so that the hardness of him pressed into her, urging her legs to part, proving to her that his need was as strong as hers.

But he still made her wait, teetering on that fine line between anguish and ecstasy.

He claimed her mouth again, capturing her tongue with his, teasing her until she almost couldn't bear it any longer. But with every fiber of her being she concentrated on the moment. Until she thought she would burst with longing.

She wrapped herself around him, kissing him hard on the mouth, all lips and tongue and take-me-right-now touches.

She loved how her curves fit perfectly into the hard angles of his body. When he moved his hands to her hips, claiming her body and pulling her closer, she arched against him, backing off to give herself enough room to slide her hand down and claim his erection. Teasing him over and over, she rubbed and stroked his desire. Until he finally put on the condom. He nudged her legs apart with his thigh and buried himself inside her.

At the rate he was going, if he didn't slow down, it would be over before he could show her exactly how much he had loved her.

Yes. He loved her.

The strangest sensation came over him.

For the first time in his life, he didn't want to run.

He had no idea where this was going, but he knew he would be here to find out.

He slowed his pace, kissing her neck as their bodies found a natural rhythm.

He was lost in the feel of her, the smell and taste of

her, until something out of place pushed its way into his awareness.

He really hadn't intended for this to happen tonight. Okay, so he'd wanted it and he was glad it had. But if he'd planned on seducing her, he would've reserved a room at the hotel.

He wanted to wait until she was ready. That was the only way this would work.

When he'd seen her standing there in front of that jackass she'd almost married, looking vulnerable and sweet and much more tempting than anyone he'd ever met in his life, he'd wondered how in the world the guy had ever let her get away. At that moment, Cullen knew he wasn't going to make the same mistake.

Still, he hadn't intended to push her to his bed. This chemistry between them was an important part of who they were together, but it was a bonus. After all she'd been through, he knew he needed to let her set the pace.

He also knew that making love to Lily couldn't just be a fling. He'd had to make sure that he was ready for it. It meant so much more and he needed to prove that to her.

He looked into her eyes as they moved together and he realized this could never be a fling. This was for keeps.

Despite the need that was driving him to the edge of insanity, once again he forced himself to slow down, taking a moment to savor how beautiful she looked and to bask in how much he loved her.

He wanted to tell her he would never hurt her. Not on purpose. Never on purpose. Knowing without a doubt the more time he spent with her, the more he knew his life was nothing without her.

Beneath the sound of blood rushing in his ears, he heard the ragged edge of her breathing become faster and stronger until she cried out.

All his senses were heightened by the sound of her pleasure, and his breathing began to match hers. He clung to her as his body thrust in and out, over and over, faster and faster until he took her over the edge of ecstasy.

Only when he was sure that she was satisfied did he allow himself to ride the mounting waves of pleasure and succumb to a final delicious thrust. A long, anguished groan erupted from his throat. He collapsed on top of her, kissing her tenderly, possessively, pulling her to him until every inch of her was pressed against him as he reveled in their spent pleasure and lost himself in the tenderness of their embrace.

Chapter Thirteen

Waking up in Cullen's arms was better than opening presents on Christmas morning, which was only four days away. Lately, though, Lily was choosing to live in the moment. Everything was still so new, and of course, they had the kids to consider.

"I think we need to be careful around the kids," she said. "They're so young they might find this confusing." She gestured back and forth between Cullen and herself.

"You're right," he said, kissing her neck. "Knowing I have to keep my hands off you is just going to make me hotter for you."

She was so comfortable in the crook of his arm she wished they could stay this way all day. However, they needed to start thinking about mobilizing, because the kids would be back at noon. It was ten o'clock.

She still had to shower and dress and make herself presentable so that the kids wouldn't notice that anything was different…although she did worry that anyone who looked at her would see her face and be able to tell that everything had changed.

"It won't be like this forever," Cullen said.

She wasn't sure what he meant exactly. Was he talking about making things permanent? As in, put-a-ring-on-it permanent? Her stomach jumped at the thought, but just as fast as the thought materialized, she shelved it. They'd known each other less than a month, and good grief, it was the morning after their first night together.

"What do you mean?" she asked.

"Cam Brady said he had some viable leads for a couple of families who might be interested in taking in the kids."

Lily's heart sank. That was the only sticky situation they hadn't worked through. She didn't want to send the kids off somewhere else. Not only had she fallen in love with him since she'd been here, but he and the kids had become her family. But that was a Pandora's box she wasn't sure she wanted to open right now. They were just getting comfortable being a couple. The other parts would work themselves out in due time.

"You're awfully quiet," he said.

She knew she needed to tread lightly, but she couldn't pretend the kids weren't important to her.

"I just can't imagine the kids not being in this house. Why are you so afraid of fatherhood? Every man I know who has kids said it's been life-changing. Sure, the lifestyle change may take some getting used to, but I've never known anyone who was an involved parent who regretted it."

She felt him pull away. It was an almost imperceptible move, but she felt it.

"The key words you just said were *involved parent*," he said. "My schedule just doesn't allow it. You've seen how many late nights I have. That wouldn't be fair to anyone."

There he was, talking in generalities again.

Whom wouldn't it be fair to? The kids? Her?

Asking might seem pushy, although she needed to know his thoughts on this sooner rather than later. Was he talking about her raising the kids and him not being an active involved parent? Because even if he wasn't talking about her specifically, she still wanted to point out that with or without the kids, whoever he was involved with would still have to endure the nights that he wasn't home.

She couldn't figure out how to make that sound right, so she went with a slight variation.

He shifted and put his arm that had been around her behind his head.

"Well, all I know is there's no such thing as a perfect situation. Life is messy and unexpected, and everyone has to compromise. If you start overthinking, it can paralyze you."

His eyebrows rose and fell, as if he were considering what she had said but was not entirely convinced.

"When I was growing up, my mother had to do it all. I was her only child, thank God. She worked and cooked and cleaned and cared for me, until I was old enough to help out. When I was old enough to see what was going on, I couldn't help thinking how horribly unfair it was that my father had been a partner in bringing me into this world but couldn't stay for the *messy parts,* as you call them.

"He was a total absentee father. He divorced my mom and came around every once in a blue moon to see me. Sometimes he'd say he'd be there, but he wouldn't show. He was so undependable and selfish that I hated him. I vowed I would never be anything like him. He was a drunk, a womanizer and basically a despicable human being. The only time he ever deigned to give me any advice, he told me that women were no good. They were only out to get knocked up and bleed you dry."

Cullen had a faraway look in his eyes and he harrumphed at something he was thinking.

Lily put her hand on his chest, drawing figure eights with the nail of her index finger. "What are you thinking?"

He looked at her and there was so much love in his eyes. "I was thinking that sometimes we don't realize how much we resemble someone. Even if we don't intend to repeat their mistakes."

Lily knew he was talking about his own broken marriage and the revolving door of women that had been a part of his own life.

"I know his marriage to my mother was bad. Before he left, I remember them screaming at each other. I know he was no prize, but I wonder if that single bad situation kept him from finding real love. Maybe he missed out on someone like you? If anything could make me feel bad for the guy, that would be it."

He leaned over, kissed her and made love to her one more time. Afterward they showered together and got ready to *go back to normal.* They had a practice run, which consisted of going downstairs and having a brunch of French toast and coffee. Lily made extra French toast for the kids and Sydney, who had even gone by to pick up George from his sleepover and was dropping him off with the girls.

"Can't you whip up a batch of the cinnamon rolls that made me fall in love with you?" Cullen said.

"Not in time for breakfast. They have to rise for two hours before I can bake them. But if you're a good boy I might be persuaded to make them for you tomorrow."

He pulled her into his arms. "Let me show you just how good I can be."

He kissed her soundly, until a knock at the front door and the persistent ring of the doorbell brought them back to reality.

The kids were home. They smiled at each other as they straightened their clothing, fixed their hair and put on their *normal* faces.

Lily answered the door while Cullen checked messages on his smartphone.

"We're back!" said Sydney as Lily welcomed them.

In a burst of exuberance, the girls were all trying to show Lily their painted nails and the temporary tattoos that Sydney, who they proclaimed was the coolest person in the world, had helped them put on.

Even George seemed a little less surly than normal.

"Did you remember I have a game today at two o'clock?" he asked.

He said this just as Cullen was coming into the living room to greet them and thank Sydney for taking the kids for the night.

Lily blinked.

Oh, boy. With everything that had been going on— baking for the holiday market, Bridget getting sick (but recovering completely in just a couple of days), preparing for the Jingle Bell Ball and figuring out her new relationship with Cullen, she had forgotten. She had even written it on the calendar, but—

"That's right," said Lily. "We're all going to be there to cheer you on."

The girls groaned about having to go.

"Basketball is boring," Megan proclaimed. "Can't we stay home?"

"It's pretty important that we all go to support George. We could be a big cheering section."

"Is Uncle Cullen going?" Bridget asked.

Lily's gaze snagged Cullen's. She gave him a look that asked, *Are you?*

"Actually I have to run by the hospital to check on a few things this morning." He hesitated. "But I'll be there as soon as I can. Would that work?"

He'd posed the question to Lily, but the girls cheered, "Yes!" in unison.

George rolled his eyes.

"What's wrong, George?" Lily asked.

"Don't tell me you're going to come if you're not."

"Hey, cut me some slack," said Cullen. He walked over and put a hand on the boy's shoulder. "I know I goofed last week, but don't I get a second chance? This is the new-and-improved Uncle Cullen, and I want to show you what I can do. I might be a little late, but I will be there. Trust me?"

"How about if he takes you out for ice cream afterward?" Lily said. "Just the two of you."

The girls protested that they wanted to go, too.

"It's not fair that he gets ice cream and we don't," Megan proclaimed.

Her declaration was supported by a pair of "Yeah"s from her little sisters.

"How about if we let the guys have some bonding time? The girls can go do something fun, too, and then we can all meet back here for dinner. Sound good?"

The question was really directed at Cullen. Looking resigned, he nodded his consent. Lily wondered if he realized that she had just shown him it was possible to be a family man.

No way in hell was Cullen going to miss this game. He set three reminders on his phone and carried around a sticky note with the word *GAME* written in big bold letters to keep him from inadvertently zoning out and being a no-show. He even excused himself from an impromptu meeting because it was edging into game time.

He arrived about fifteen minutes late, but that was okay because he'd told the boy he would be late. And when George saw him his face visibly brightened and he started moving the ball with more hustle.

He was actually a pretty good player, Cullen thought. Who knew? Maybe he and the boy could set up a backboard out back—but then he remembered that the kids would be leaving shortly after Christmas.

But they probably would come to visit. So maybe a hoop wasn't completely out of the question.

Cullen found Lily and the girls and sat with them, and they all cheered for George and his team. The last fifteen minutes of the game, the score was neck and neck. It was a one-point game, so every basket mattered. George's team would score and the other team would take the ball right back down the court and answer it with another basket. So much for defense, Cullen thought, but maybe he'd work with the boy on that. Maybe George would end up playing ball in high school. For a couple of minutes Cullen imagined him and Lily going to watch all the home games and introducing them to his friends as his aunt Lily and uncle Cullen.

He glanced at Lily, trying on the fantasy.

While he looked away, something happened on the court. George and the kid from the other team were tussling over the ball. Each boy had a grip on it in a last-minute showdown. They were yanking on it so hard that the two boys were nearly standing in a circle trying to gain possession.

George's team led by one point. The small crowd got to its feet.

Cullen, Lily and the girls cheered, "Go, George, go! Get the ball."

As if bolstered by the support, George gave one quick, decisive yank and jerked the ball free. Holding it to his chest, he hesitated for a second, looking up in the stands. He made eye contact with Cullen, who cheered wildly.

"That's my boy! Way to go! You got this."

Even though his team had the lead, it would be so great for his confidence if he could score the final basket. According to Lily, last night's sleepover with some of the guys on the team had been a breakthrough of sorts. George was making friends and showing so much confidence out on the court.

Then, as if it happened in slow motion, George took off running. The wrong way. He was running the wrong way down the court. The crowd was yelling again. Cullen was trying to get his attention to tell him to turn around and go the other way. Even if he held on to the ball until the clock ran out, his team would win, but George seemed to be so caught up in the frenzy that he shot the ball at the basket and scored the final two points for the other team.

Lily reached out and took ahold of Cullen's hand and whispered, "Oh, boy. Oh, no."

The opposing team won the match by one point.

For a split second the entire gymnasium went absolutely silent. George's teammates stood stock-still on the court, gaping at him in disbelief.

Then the guys on the other team broke out into a frenzy of cheers and applause, exhibiting terrible sportsmanship. They jeered at George and slapped high fives with each other as they taunted George for winning the game for them. Wasn't someone going to stop them? Someone really needed to sit them down and talk to them about that. In fact, in all fairness, shouldn't they forfeit the basket because of unsportsmanlike behavior?

But the damage had already been done. That would only bring more attention to George's error.

Cullen turned to Lily. "Why don't you go ahead and take the girls home? I'll go get George and try to do some damage control."

"Are you sure?" Lily asked him.

"Yes, I've got this." He was driven by an incredibly overwhelming sense of protectiveness. A long time ago, he had been the kid on the team who made the mistake and there was no one there to stand up for him. His mom had been working and his dad was nowhere to be found. Cullen had been left to fend for himself. It was the worst feeling in the world for a little boy.

Cullen knew he might not be father material, but this, *this* was personal.

As Lily ushered the girls from the gymnasium, Cullen made his way down to the court to retrieve George, who was still standing frozen underneath the basket.

"Hey, buddy," he said. "How about we go get that banana split we talked about?"

Where was the coach? Cullen wanted to tear into him right now for not being there to reinforce that it was just a game and George had done the best he could do. Hell, George had been doing a great job till the end. This was the kind of thing that could scar a kid for life. It could make him turn inward—or push him further inward than he already was.

One of the refs was shuffling some papers and for a split second Cullen considered going over and tearing him a new one for letting the boys on the other team get away with acting the way they did. Then he looked at George, who was standing there staring into space as if he weren't completely there.

The best thing he could do for the boy was get him the hell out of there. Three minutes later the two of them were buckled into Cullen's car, pulling out of the community center, leaving the bad memory in the dust. Maybe not immediately, but the faster he got the kid the ice cream, the sooner George would see that the errant basket didn't matter.

As he pointed the car in the direction of Polar Bear Ice Cream, Cullen pondered what to say. Should he start with how wrong the boys on the other team had been to act the way they did? Or no, maybe a softer approach about this just being a game, not brain surgery—ha-ha, a little medical humor? But no, that would seem to trivialize it.

Damn it, why was this so hard?

They'd been on the road for five minutes when the boy leaned over and buried his head in Cullen's shoulder and began to sob.

Cullen's mind went completely blank. He sat there for a good two minutes with both hands gripping the steering wheel as the boy blubbered.

There were no words that would talk him out of that state of mind. Now that he was away from the guys on the team and the sting of what happened had set in, Cullen decided it was probably best just to let the boy cry it out.

Unsure if it was the right thing to do, but not having any other ideas, Cullen eased one arm around the boy and clumsily patted his right shoulder.

Less than two minutes later they approached Polar Bear Ice Cream, but before Cullen could turn in the drive, he noticed some of the boys from George's team were there.

Nope. Not a good idea. Thank God George hadn't seen them because he had his face buried in Cullen's armpit, crying at a steady convulsive sob.

Cullen drove right past the place and before he knew it he was on the open road headed toward Dallas.

Sometimes it was just better to get out of town where nobody knew you until you could get yourself together.

They got to Dallas about twenty minutes later and drove around with no particular destination in mind for another half hour. Finally George lifted his head and scooted back over. Cullen returned his right hand to the steering wheel and turned the car in the direction of Celebration.

Before they made it to the main highway, Cullen

spied a fast-food restaurant ahead. Without a word, he steered the car into the restaurant's drive-through.

"What flavor shake do you want?" he asked the boy.

"Chocolate."

He ordered two large chocolate shakes. When they were ready he handed one to the boy, fixed one for himself and they nursed them all the way home.

Neither one said a word, but by the time they were home George's eyes were no longer red. He'd blown his nose on one of the napkins that they'd gotten at the restaurant. No one would be the wiser about his emotions.

His secret was safe with Cullen. Except that he would tell Lily. He had to tell Lily—in case he was somehow damaging the boy by not encouraging him to talk about his emotions.

God, this parenthood gig wasn't for amateurs.

Milk-shake cups in hand, the two got out of the car and started toward the front door. Halfway up the walk, George stopped. Cullen thought maybe the kid had left something in the car. He was ready to toss him the keys when George threw his arms around Cullen's waist and hugged him hard. It nearly knocked Cullen off balance, it was so unexpected.

"That's all we said the entire time we were out," Cullen said to Lily once the children were in bed and they had a chance to talk about the day's turn of events over a glass of wine. "I don't know why he hugged me. I didn't do anything to help him. The only words we exchanged the entire time we were out were *What flavor shake do you want?* And *Chocolate.*

"What should I have said or done to help him? I should've *done* something."

Lily reached out and took his hand. He laced his fingers through hers and held on tight.

"But you did do something," she said. "Sometimes less is more. Sometimes showing up is all you need to do."

She instantly regretted the words as soon as they'd slipped from her lips. Maybe talking about *showing up* hit too close to home after he'd shared the bad situation with his father. He'd been so bent on DNA and his father's bad traits being in his genes. Maybe she shouldn't have brought it up when emotions were so raw like right now.

"Unfortunately kids don't come with an instruction manual. You just have to go with your gut. See, you have good instincts."

He shook his head. She couldn't tell if he was traumatized or maybe a little shocked and in awe of himself.

"I couldn't do this on a regular basis," he said.

Lily squinted at him. "Are you serious? You really don't want kids?"

Rather than answer, Cullen picked up his wineglass and took a long pull.

"I have to be honest with you. That's a...a deal breaker for me. Not only do I want kids, I want a bunch of them. You were an only child, too. Don't you regret not having siblings?"

He whistled through his teeth and shook his head. "As hard as my mother had to work to put food on the table and keep a roof over our heads? And she only had one. There's no way. No way I could do this with a whole brood."

"You judge how you would be by the way your father was. In fact, it seems like it would make you even more determined to be the kind of father you wish he would have been. You're stable, Cullen. You have so much to offer and these kids really need you."

He shook his head again, looking beleaguered, sort of like she'd backed him into a corner.

"It doesn't matter. Look at Greg. He had everything in the world going for him. He still ended up letting down his kids."

Lily snorted. "Because he had the audacity to die? I mean, sure, it's a sad situation—my own parents died when I was ten years old. I certainly don't mean to make light of it, but we're all going to die someday, Cullen. You can't stop living because you're afraid to die."

"I'm not afraid of death. I guess I've never seen myself being a father. Look, it's been a long day. I don't think we should be having this conversation now."

"If not now, when, Cullen? I think we need to talk about it sooner rather than later."

When he didn't answer, she said, "We need to give this some major thought. I don't know if we're going to work, because it looks to me like we want completely different lives."

Chapter Fourteen

For the next two and a half days, Cullen threw himself into work. With so many things going for them, how could he and Lily have reached such an impasse? But to have children or not to have them was a fundamental decision for a couple. It was part of the foundation that their relationship was built on.

With Lily, it had been love at first sight. He had never experienced it before and frankly he didn't expect it to happen again. Sure, he could probably find someone or many someones down the road. But they wouldn't be Lily. Why did they have to have a fundamental difference as large as the Grand Canyon threatening to keep them apart?

Was it fair to expect her to sacrifice having kids of her own? For God's sake, she was a teacher. Kids were her calling. But was it any better to go against his own nature?

As he was turning off his computer, his gaze fell on a picture that Hannah had drawn for him with very strict instructions that he was to take it to work because this picture was for his desk. He'd done it, too. Here it was, front and center on his desk as if it meant something to him.

The drawing must have meant something to him. Otherwise it would still be in the car or would have gotten lost en route. But he'd never really looked at it.

He picked up the piece of notebook paper and examined it. It was a rudimentary drawing of a house with a red front door and smoke coming out of the chimney. A bunch of stick figures stood in front of the house. She'd drawn four females—or so he guessed they were females judging by the triangles that seemed to represent skirts and bows in their hair. Next to them were two more figures, unadorned except for the big smiles that took up the majority of their faces. Those must be guys.

Picture in hand, Cullen leaned back in his chair.

Four girls and two guys. It was obviously a depiction of Cullen and Lily with the kids. The hands of the tallest female and male stick figures intersected. Had she drawn them holding hands?

She was a smart girl. She'd probably picked up on more than Lily realized.

He could hear Lily saying, *Kids are more perceptive than you think.*

Obviously.

He returned the picture to its place on his desk and finished shutting down his computer. It was Christmas Eve, and he was working only until noon. Now that he and Lily had a chance to cool off and think rationally, he'd planned on taking the rest of the day off and spending it with them.

It had snowed last night, covering everything with a fluffy blanket of white. After he finished his Christmas shopping, he intended to track Lily and the kids outside to build a snowman. It was Christmas Eve. Today they would put aside their differences and just be together.

He grabbed his phone, his keys and his coat, wished merry Christmas to the skeleton crew that was making time and a half working the holiday and headed out.

He was waiting for the elevator when his cell phone rang. The name Cameron Brady, the family-law attorney he'd hired, flashed on the display.

"Merry Christmas, Cam. Are you working on Christmas Eve, too?"

"Merry Christmas to you, too, Cullen. I'm always working. No rest for the weary and all that hogwash. Listen, I'm calling with semi-good news. It's not exactly the big present from Santa that the kids are hoping for, but it's a start. I wanted to run it by you and see what you think."

"What do you have for me, Cam?"

Elevator doors opened, but Cullen turned around and walked back to his office, where he could talk to Cam privately.

"Like I said, it's not exactly the news you were hoping for, but I've found a family that is interested in adopting the two youngest girls."

Cullen watched the snow fall from his office window as he digested the attorney's words.

"The family lives in Oklahoma City. That's about a three-hour drive from Celebration."

"They're not interested in taking all four? Keeping them together is a priority."

"Right, but so was placing them before the school session reconvenes after the holidays. Right now this is the best I can do. We might be able to find an Oklahoma-based foster family that's willing to take in the older two. But at least the younger two will be settled by the first of the year and won't have to be uprooted after they start school."

Cullen was silent. What was he supposed to say? "This isn't optimum, Cam."

The attorney heaved a weary sigh. "I know, I know. But I have to level with you, Cullen. It's a long shot thinking you're going to find a family that will take all four of them. More than a long shot. It's pretty close to impossible. At least with the time constraints. If you're willing to keep them or put them in foster care while we search, that's a different story. Even so, it's not an easy row to hoe.

"Why don't you think about it, or talk to the kids, see how they feel about it and give me a call back? Kids are resilient."

"Thanks, Cam. I'll be in touch."

The snow was falling like tears from heaven when Cullen hung up the phone. If he thought having kids was difficult, making the decision whether or not to give them up was excruciating.

He was damned if he did and damned if he didn't. And to think it had all started with an off-the-cuff promise to a little girl. Now their fate was in his hands.

What kind of Christmas would it be if he told the kids he was splitting them up? They would be devastated and Lily would never forgive him. But this decision was about what was best for the kids.

The only thing he knew for sure was that he was going to wait until after Christmas to tell them. He wanted them to have this holiday as a family, without any added stress or sadness. It was the least he could do.

On Christmas morning, the six of them gathered around the Christmas tree. Lily had taken care to set out Santa's presents and wrap the remaining gifts as beautifully as possible. She'd purchased several small gifts for each child so the tree would look festive and the kids would have fun opening lots of presents.

She and Cullen had been like ships passing each other since their conversation on Sunday. He'd been gone a lot, which made it easier. She didn't see how this was going to end any other way than badly.

She was glad he was willing to wait until after Christmas for them to have the talk. Today, she put on a cheerful face. She was going to make darn sure neither of them tripped over the elephant in the room.

She'd even gotten him a Christmas present. A crystal decanter etched with his initials. He hadn't been easy to buy for. What in the world did you get a man who had everything?

Everything except the main thing he needed.

But that wasn't her call. The last thing she wanted to do was force him into saying that he wanted children when he didn't. That would be worse than the marriage ultimatum she'd leveled on Josh.

She finally got it. She saw the writing on the wall clearly. Two people had to come to a meeting of the minds before they could be happy as a couple. You couldn't strong-arm somebody into important life decisions. Because the heart wanted what the heart wanted. And sometimes there was just no getting around fundamental differences.

The sad thing was, her heart still wanted Cullen.

She might have made a conscious decision to live with her eyes wide-open, but mending her heart would be a long, slow process. That was fine because once the kids were placed in a permanent home and she went back to her regular teaching job, she would have all the time in the world to put herself back together again.

She feared, though, that all the parts might not fit back together the way they were before she met Cullen and the kids.

Then again, she wasn't the same person she was before meeting them.

"Who wants to play Santa?" she asked in her cheeriest voice. All four kids raised their hands. "How about this? How about if each one of you gets to deliver a round of presents?"

Megan stood. "And I get to go first because I'm the oldest."

Cullen set down his mug of coffee. "Actually before going by age, I think I'm the oldest. So I'll go first."

Megan groaned, but she sat back down with her brother and sisters.

Lily was glad that Cullen was giving out presents first.

If he hadn't gotten her anything, it would be less awkward for her to give him his present later.

She didn't give presents to get them. But they were in such flux right now that she wasn't sure what she should do. She loved giving gifts. Actually she liked giving them even more than she enjoyed receiving them. So she had purchased the decanter and she'd wrapped it with the same love and care that she'd wrapped the other packages.

Really, it was fine if he hadn't gotten her anything.

"I have a special present for everyone," he said. "And I mean everyone."

The kids clapped their hands, giddy with anticipation.

"How about if we start with Franklin?"

"Huh?" George couldn't hide his surprise. "Even Franklin gets a present?"

The dog, who was lying next to Hannah, lifted his shaggy head at the sound of his name.

"Yes," said Cullen. "Even Franklin. His is outside in the backyard. Shall we go see it?"

The kids, who were clad in their flannel Christmas pajamas—another gift from Lily—got to their feet and ran toward the back door.

"Put your shoes and coats on," Lily insisted. "It's cold outside."

"Yes," Cullen agreed. "Listen to Lily, please. It's cold out there."

He even managed a nervous-looking smile.

Good. The elephant wouldn't be in the way today.

That would be the best Christmas present.

Once everyone had donned their coats, scarves and shoes, Cullen led the way out into the backyard, where a doghouse with a big red bow on it sat in the side yard.

"Look what you got, Franklin," cried Hannah. "It's a house just for you."

It was nice, but it was an odd gift given the circumstances. But if Cullen had been able to transport it from the pet store or wherever he'd gotten it, then the kids would be able to transport it to their new home so Franklin could use it wherever they ended up.

The thought made Lily sad, but she reframed her thoughts and decided that maybe it would be as though they were taking a piece of this home with them to their new home.

"Okay, who should be next?" he asked, tapping his finger on his chin, pretending to put a lot of thought into the decision.

The kids loved it. They jumped up and down, raising their hands and shouting, "Me! Me! Me!"

"All of you can all go next," he said. "But you have to follow me."

He marched them around to the other side of the house, where a large blue tarp covered a surprise.

"And now if my lovely assistant, Lily, would be so gracious as to help me with the unveiling?"

Lovely?

At least he was playing nice. More than nice, actually. He was treating the kids quite wonderfully, and her heart swelled as it had gotten into the habit of doing whenever Cullen simply acted like himself.

If he could only see himself through her eyes, he would see what a great father he would be.

Once again, she reframed her thoughts. "I would be happy to help you, good sir."

The kids laughed at her exaggerated assistant impression.

She went to the other end of the tarp and lifted the edge, just as Cullen was doing on his end.

"On the count of three, please," he said. "One, two, *three!*"

Together they lifted the tarp with as much flourish as they could manage and revealed the six bicycles, complete with helmets, hidden underneath.

Bicycles? He'd gotten them bicycles.

And he'd gotten one for himself and her, too?

There was more hooting and hollering from the kids as they scrambled over to choose their bikes.

After the excitement settled, and all the kids were astride their respective bikes, George asked, "Will we be able to take our bikes and Franklin's new house with us when we move in with our new family?"

"Oh, George, buddy, I don't think you should take the bikes anywhere else," Cullen said.

It broke Lily's heart to watch the kids' faces fall.

Really? Couldn't he have gotten them something a little less expensive or a little more portable than bikes if he didn't want them to take them when they left?

Rather than reframing, she chewed on this one for a moment, deciding that she would argue the case for the kids to take the bikes. What was he going to do with six bikes?

Cullen must have noticed how fast the fun barometer had fallen, because he quickly added, "There's a reason for that, and it's the best Christmas present of all. Are you ready for it?"

The kids found their smiles again, but they looked a little hesitant, still probably stuck on the part about not taking the bikes anywhere else.

"Everybody gather around," he said, motioning them toward him. "Come on. You can get back on the bikes later. This is important. So come on."

The kids complied, giving wistful looks to the bicycles as they dismounted and joined Cullen's huddle. Lily hung back watching the bittersweet scene.

"Is everyone here?" Cullen asked. He made a show of counting heads. "One, two, three, four, five. We're missing someone. Who are we missing?"

"Lily!" the kids shouted.

"Lily," Cullen repeated. "Lily, huddle up."

The way he smiled at her made her heart break all over again. Even so, she complied.

Cullen made room for her in the circle next to him. He put his arm around her and pulled her in.

She refused to think about how perfectly their bodies fit together, even at something playful like this.

"Are you ready?" Cullen asked once everyone was present and accounted for. "I have fabulous news. I found a family for you, right here in Celebration."

The kids' eyes grew large.

"And we can all stay together?" Megan asked, concern clouding her blue eyes.

"Absolutely," said Cullen. "Because you are all going to stay right here. I mean, if that's okay with you."

The kids jumped up and down and clapped their hands, cheering even louder than before.

Lily gasped and clapped and cheered right along with them.

When? What? When had he decided to do a complete one-eighty? The last time they'd talked about it… Well, he wouldn't even talk about it. But it didn't matter; she was so happy for him and the kids. She tried not to let herself dwell on what it meant for the two of them and their relationship. Still, she couldn't help wondering.

After the excitement died down, and they managed to drag the kids away from the cold and from their new bikes, with the promise of an after-dinner bike ride, a completely different thought struck Lily.

Before they reconvened around the Christmas tree, Lily said, "I'm so happy for you and the kids. Have you given any thought about where they'll go to school? If you send them to Brighton Academy, I'd be happy to help you take them to and from school. But I just need to make sure that you realize I'm going back to work after the first of the year. I can't be your full-time nanny."

Cullen reached out and ran a finger over her bottom lip. "I don't want you to be the nanny. I want you to be my wife."

Lily blinked once. Then twice. Unsure if she'd heard him right. "Cullen?"

"I realize this is sudden and I'm hoping you don't think I got carried away. I probably should've talked to you about this before telling the kids—"

"No," she said. "This is the most wonderful Christmas present you could've given them. You've given them a home, Cullen."

Her eyes welled with tears from the beauty of it all.

"I love you, Lily. You and the kids are the only real family I've ever known. It took a while for me to realize it, but I can't imagine living another day without you."

He told her about the call he'd gotten from Cameron Brady. "After talking to him and facing the prospect of splitting the kids up and them not getting the chance to grow up together, I just couldn't do it. It all became crystal clear. The kids had to stay with me. And there's one more thing."

He took her hand and led her into the living room, where the kids were gathered around the Christmas tree.

"Lily gets the next present," he said. He reached down and pulled a small box from under the tree skirt. Holding her hand, he got down on one knee and presented the box to her.

"Lily Palmer, will you do me the honor of being my wife?"

"Please say yes," said Bridget. "Then you can be our mommy rather than our nanny."

Lily was so overcome with emotion, she was stunned speechless. Cullen must've mistaken the look on her face for hesitation because he said, "Kids, why don't you go out and look at your new bikes for a few moments? Then after you come back in, we'll finish opening presents."

The kids ran to the back door.

Lily finally found her voice. "You didn't have to send them outside."

"Yes, I did. I need you to know that I love you. I want to marry you because I want a life with you, not just because you would be a convenient nanny for the kids. However, when I decided to adopt them, I made the decision to commit fully to them, too.

"I wanted to make a big gesture so that you know how much you mean to me. I'm willing to fight for you to make you stay. But I didn't realize how daunting this all must be for you. If you need time to think about it, I understand."

"Cullen, are you trying to talk me into marrying you or are you trying to talk me out of it?"

"No. Neither. I mean, yes. I would be the happiest man in the world if you would marry me."

"Yes. My answer is yes. Because I can't imagine living a day without you, either. All of you."

He pulled her into his arms and kissed her senseless.

"Let's go get the kids," he said.

When they were all together around the tree, he got down on one knee again and took her hand. "I want this to be right. So, I'm going to ask again. Will you do me the great honor of being my wife?"

"Yes! That would make me the happiest woman in the world."

Cullen took the ring from the box—a gorgeous round solitaire that winked in the light of the Christmas tree— and slipped it on her finger. It fit perfectly. Just like her new family.

Before Cullen could get to his feet, George sneaked up between him and Lily and held a piece of mistletoe between them.

"Now you have to kiss," Megan said, jumping up and down, clapping her hands. "If you don't, you'll be breaking the rules of Christmas."

* * * * *

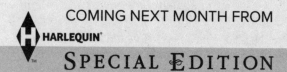

COMING NEXT MONTH FROM

HARLEQUIN®

SPECIAL EDITION

Available November 18, 2014

YOU CAN FIND MORE INFORMATION ON UPCOMING HARLEQUIN® TITLES, FREE EXCERPTS AND MORE AT WWW.HARLEQUIN.COM.

HSECNM1114

REQUEST YOUR FREE BOOKS!

2 FREE NOVELS PLUS 2 FREE GIFTS!

⬡ HARLEQUIN®

SPECIAL EDITION

Life, Love & Family

YES! Please send me 2 FREE Harlequin® Special Edition novels and my 2 FREE gifts (gifts are worth about $10). After receiving them, if I don't wish to receive any more books, I can return the shipping statement marked "cancel." If I don't cancel, I will receive 6 brand-new novels every month and be billed just $4.74 per book in the U.S. or $5.24 per book in Canada. That's a savings of at least 14% off the cover price! It's quite a bargain! Shipping and handling is just 50¢ per book in the U.S. and 75¢ per book in Canada.* I understand that accepting the 2 free books and gifts places me under no obligation to buy anything. I can always return a shipment and cancel at any time. Even if I never buy another book, the two free books and gifts are mine to keep forever.

235/335 HDN F45Y

Name	(PLEASE PRINT)	
Address		Apt. #
City	State/Prov.	Zip/Postal Code

Signature (if under 18, a parent or guardian must sign)

Mail to the Harlequin® Reader Service:
IN U.S.A.: P.O. Box 1867, Buffalo, NY 14240-1867
IN CANADA: P.O. Box 609, Fort Erie, Ontario L2A 5X3

Want to try two free books from another line?
Call 1-800-873-8635 or visit www.ReaderService.com.

* Terms and prices subject to change without notice. Prices do not include applicable taxes. Sales tax applicable in N.Y. Canadian residents will be charged applicable taxes. Offer not valid in Quebec. This offer is limited to one order per household. Not valid for current subscribers to Harlequin Special Edition books. All orders subject to credit approval. Credit or debit balances in a customer's account(s) may be offset by any other outstanding balance owed by or to the customer. Please allow 4 to 6 weeks for delivery. Offer available while quantities last.

Your Privacy—The Harlequin® Reader Service is committed to protecting your privacy. Our Privacy Policy is available online at www.ReaderService.com or upon request from the Harlequin Reader Service.

We make a portion of our mailing list available to reputable third parties that offer products we believe may interest you. If you prefer that we not exchange your name with third parties, or if you wish to clarify or modify your communication preferences, please visit us at www.ReaderService.com/consumerchoice or write to us at Harlequin Reader Service Preference Service, P.O. Box 9062, Buffalo, NY 14269. Include your complete name and address.

HSE13R

***

The whole time he worked, he was aware of her—the pure blue of her eyes, her skin, dusted with pink from the cold, the soft curves as she reached over her head to hand him the end of the light string.

"That should do it for me," he said after a moment. In more ways than one.

"Good work. Should we plug them in so we can see how they look?"

"Sure."

She went inside the little structure at the entrance to the village, where she must have flipped a few switches. They had finished only about half, but the cottages with lights indeed looked magical against the pearly twilight spreading across the landscape as the sun set.

"Ahhh. Beautiful," she exclaimed. "I never get tired of that."

"Truly lovely," he agreed, though he was looking at her and not the cottages.

She smiled at him. "I'm sorry you gave up your whole afternoon to help me, but the truth is I would have been sunk without you. Thank you."

"You're welcome. I can finish these up when I get here in the morning, after I take Joey to school. Now that I've sort of figured out what I'm doing, I should be able to get these lights hung in no time and start work on the repairs at the Lodge by midmorning."

She smiled at him again, a bright, vibrant smile that made his heart pound as if he had just raced up to the top of those mountains up there and back.

"You are the best Christmas present ever, Rafe. Seriously."

He raised an eyebrow. "Am I?"

He didn't mean the words to sound like innuendo but he was almost certain that sudden flush on her cheeks had nothing to do with the cool November air.

"You know what I mean."

He did. She was talking about his help around the ranch. He was taken by surprise by a sudden fierce longing that her words should mean something completely different.

"I'm not sure I've ever been anyone's favorite Christmas gift before," he murmured.

She gave him a sidelong look. "Then it's about time, isn't it?"

***

Hope Nichols was never able to find her place in the world—until her family's Colorado holiday attraction, the Christmas Ranch, faces closure. This Christmas, she's determined to rescue the ranch with the help of handsome former Navy SEAL Rafe Santiago and his adorable nephew. As sparks fly between mysterious Rafe and Hope, this Christmas will be one that nobody in Cold Creek will ever forget!

Don't miss THE CHRISTMAS RANCH
available December 2014, wherever
Harlequin® Special Edition books and ebooks are sold!